# The Goose and The Crone

*Best Wishes*
*Joyce :*
*Denise White*

## Denise A White

authorHOUSE®

*AuthorHouse™*
*1663 Liberty Drive*
*Bloomington, IN 47403*
*www.authorhouse.com*
*Phone: 1-800-839-8640*

*First published by AuthorHouse 4/18/2011*

*ISBN: 978-1-4520-8633-0 (sc)*

*Printed in the United States of America*

*This book is printed on acid-free paper.*

*Certain stock imagery © Thinkstock.*

# The Crone

Mend

Healing, free choices

Head merrily down the path

Positively free

-Elizabeth Washburn, from her book Wisdom Walking

# Chapter 1

Elizabeth waved to her friend as she held her destiny in her hand.

. . .

The 55 degree water she swam in reflected the color of the sky and together they appeared to form one large turquoise stone flawed only by a vein of tree lined branches on the horizon. And as she emerged from her early morning swim, the cold morning air made her skin pebble. "This will be a good work day," she said loudly to the land. Then, wrapping herself in a warm blanket while pulling on a pair of old sweatpants, she went gingerly up the hill.

After a breakfast of brown-sugared oatmeal, she dressed in khakis and a tee shirt ready to start her day. Elizabeth slipped her arms into a black and red wool work shirt with the cuffs frayed from many years of loving wear. The well-worn leather gloves were always in her slightly ripped pocket, as were the set of keys she would need for the pole barn. After lacing up her steel-toed work boots, she went out the door grabbing a floppy hiking-type hat to cover her snow white hair. Her yellow seated tractor, waiting just inside those doors, made Elizabeth know all was right with the world.

"Yes," Elizabeth said to her shadow, "today **will be** a good work day."

. . .

Elizabeth's turnkey cabin had been built on three levels in the late 60's. Elizabeth and Carl, her husband, had finished off the modified A-frame with redwood paneling. There was the main room, with its floor to ceiling field stone fireplace, a loft, a bedroom, a bathroom, and a walkout basement. The basement held a workshop and a place to store

Carl's tractor at that time. But upon retirement, from fifty-nine years of city lights and thirty-six years of teaching, Elizabeth had remodeled it. There was a spa, sauna, and a small wood burning stove. The reason for all of this, though Elizabeth would never admit it, was to have a fireside view, for a romantic interlude, in the spa. Elizabeth always laughed out loud at the thought! That was ten years ago.

The home, no longer just a cabin, was at the end of a private road. The road, one she, her husband, and her parents, had created from the woods, took almost fifteen minutes to walk even now. With a twinkle in her bright blue eyes, usually around the fire pit, on a crisp fall evening, Elizabeth would tell the creation story to her friends.

"It was the winter of 1968," she would say. "Mom and Dad, Carl and I had started for the property early in the morning with the trunk of the old Pontiac loaded. We had our shovels, chain saws, and one large brush wacker. With every bump we hit bottom. There were about three inches of snow on the road; what little progress we had made in clearing to road before needed to be cleared again before we could proceed any further. We were able to drive as far as the Mickerson's when a large drift halted us in our tracks and we had to abandon the car entirely. The shoveling was going along quite smoothly when all of a sudden Mom wavered and stepped off the road trying to get her balance back. The silence was broken by a yell for help, as if someone was drowning! There she was flailing her arms about like a vertical snow angel. She was sunk up to her hips in powder. It took three of us, shoveling and pulling, to get her 4'11" body out of that drift. As soon as she was out, however, she brushed herself off, picked up her shovel, and went right on working as if nothing had ever happened!"

The road, when finished, ended at what Elizabeth thought of as her northern Wisconsin lake. It opened its eyes to reveal over 1500 feet of lake shore. Elizabeth was also blessed with 25 acres of wooded land and all the wildlife it held. A trail, used in all seasons for hiking or snow shoeing or cross-country skiing, had been cut by her and her friend, Sarah, in the 80's. Sarah had said to Elizabeth on Sept. 17, 1985, "Come on 'Woodswoman', you've had your day." With that statement the path was finished. This, of course became another of Elizabeth's stories.

The grandiose pole barn, made of timber and steel, sat 100 yards opposite the house. Such buildings were used widely up north for storage. Elizabeth's was filled with her tractor, trailer, boat, snowmobiles, tools,

2

and storage boxes. The pole barn was as neat as a pin: snowmobiles were on the left, one behind the other, tractor and trailer on the right, boat in the middle, boxes on shelves, tools around the perimeter, and truck in back of the boat. Above the rafters, rays of light came in. There, the humming birds came to rest in the summer; some to die, but most gently encouraged out by Elizabeth.

. . .

Elizabeth went into the pole barn, placed her ample body on the smoothly worn, yellow seat, slid the choke just past the rabbit and turned the key twice. It always needed an extra crank, like Elizabeth, herself. She drove it out and the leaves crunched and the twigs snapped as the tractor came to rest in its precisely cut parking place. As the sun turned up the heat, Elizabeth removed her outer shirt. She moved her foot off the clutch and brake, and the tractor lurched forward and headed for the large wood pile. The pile of wood sat five or six yards from the porch door. The wood, cut and dried for a year, had been ready to split a couple of weeks ago. There was birch, poplar, pine, and oak. The soft wood was separated from the hard wood and the long lengths separated from the short ones.

As she looked at the wood pile, Elizabeth fondly remembered one year when the pile had been stacked. It was Thanksgiving and Sarah and her parents, Alan and Ann Belmond, had been there for the holiday.

Elizabeth could hear Alan now, "We've come to 'make wood' Elizabeth, for our dinner. I haven't done it since I was a young man and left the farm. I brought my gloves. When do we start?"

"We can start as soon as I've fed you. Come give me a hug. It's so good to see you," she had called back.

Sarah and Elizabeth had split the wood earlier in the fall but due to the volume, from a particularly large windfall that summer, could not get it all stacked. So in the cold of a late Thanksgiving afternoon, Alan, Ann, and Sarah helped finish the time-consuming task of wood stacking.

The wood, laying haphazardly by the pole barn, was loaded into the truck and driven to the wood pile. Forming an assembly line, the friends grabbed, and passed, and stacked the wood. Then, Elizabeth *neatly* placed the long lengths, for the field stone fireplace, in one pile, with the soft and hard woods separated, and then the shorter lengths likewise, for the stove in the basement, in another pile.

Sarah stood in the bed of the truck, Alan and Ann caught her wood and gently passed it to Elizabeth. They continued almost nonstop for 2 or three hours, except for Ann, who was always blowing her leaky-faucet nose. Of course everyone counted on her because she always had tissue up her sleeve or in a pocket.

There was a Polaroid snapshot in Elizabeth's mind of the occasion. She had on her usual clothing: khakis and red wool shirt over her long underwear (which of course no one could see) and various other layers of clothing, her floppy hat with earmuffs underneath and her lined leather gloves. About the only skin revealed were her chubby cheeks and nose; both being quite red from the biting cold that had settled in when the shadows had become long. Sarah looked like a lumberjack in her plaid wool shirt, boots, lined leather gloves, and a toque. All of these and more, including wool socks for her frostbite prone feet, adorned her body. Alan was the deer hunter in Elizabeth's blaze-orange, hooded sweatshirt over his many layers and his own lined work gloves. Then there was the misfit, as there always is in a family picture. Elizabeth's mind snapped the picture and there stood Ann as she appeared; in her long brown wool coat, blue polyester pants peeking out below, knitted gray gloves, and a kerchief tied around her head.

As the sun had set over the lake that day, and the warmth of the fire soaked into their bones, the turkey and mayo sandwiches completed the perfect story.

"What wonderful memories," Elizabeth said to herself and smiled.

• • •

The full-sized GM truck had long since been traded for a Chevy S-10 with a topper, so now all she had was her John Deere with its trailer to move the wood. Elizabeth drove the tractor over to the pole barn and attached the trailer. "Well, it will take a few more trips, that's all, and what is there but time," Elizabeth smiled as she talked to the tractor.

Earlier, the log holder had been moved near the basement door. She loaded short lengths of hard and soft wood into the trailer and descended the hill in 2nd gear, jostling in her seat in rhythm with the logs in the back.

"Jumpin' jiminy, this road is getting mighty rough!" she cried out loud as she flew off the seat a few inches and the tractor shut off. "I better take it more slowly."

So back and forth, up and down the hill she went until the wood was cleanly stacked. "Now, when winter comes and I need that extra burst of heat while I soak in the spa, I can load the wood-burning stove down here without navigating any stairs. That will be a blessing to my knees."

# Lattice

I acknowledge me

on so many living planes

universal web

-Elizabeth Washburn, from her book <u>Wisdom Walking</u>

# Chapter 2

Pahaana, her light skinned brothers, had written a book on which Elizabeth's father had relied, *The Farmers Almanac*. It was indispensable to many of his generation because it predicted when winter would come in a particular year. However, she made her predictions based on the signs: when geese headed south, how wide the black stripe on the woolly caterpillars were, when the acorns fell from the oak trees, or the size of the ring around the moon. She lived the teachings of her mother's ancestors.

Elizabeth had been absorbed with thoughts of an early winter: geese, acorns, caterpillars and the ring of the October moon, when she began to think of all the fall chores still left to be done before the season ahead. Fall chores and activities had to be started earlier each year due to arthritis, her main adversary. It had come to stay and was quite belligerent in the cold months. The decision to become a snowbird, like her friends, was bearing down like a train once again. Would she finally jump track and let her bones bask in the warmth of the sun? Or was the beauty of warmth found in the palette of fall enough to last until spring?

• • •

Her days were full now, so full it was hard for her aging body to meet her mind's daily goals. She looked at the list in front of her.

1. stacking split dried wood; done
2. window wells
3. leaves: rake, bag, burn, distribute
4. fence flower gardens
5. pull annuals
6. snowmobiles

7. pull batteries: cycles, boat
8. winter maintenance-John Deere
   a. change oil, plugs
   b. mowing deck
   c. leaf attachment
   d. clean snow blower & check
9. take in dock
10. remove pump from lake; put aerator in
11. turn outside water off, bring in hose
12. clean and drain spa

. . .

Dragging out the window wells from the shelf in the pole barn took all her strength, steel was so much heavier than plastic. These worked perfectly fine, though, and besides they had been her fathers. She had eight to put on. That meant eight trips from the edge of the yard on foot.

Elizabeth worked meticulously as she went from one basement window to the next. She cleaned leaves away from each window before installing the window well. Her back throbbed like the thud of the bass coming from an overpowered car stereo. She'd had to take several 'stand up' breaks from her work rolling her body upward as if rolling up a window against the offending noise.

After working about a half hour she had all the wells in place. The first had only taken minutes to carry but she could barely drag the last one over. Driving the tractor would have been better but it would have been like a steel ball on a pin ball machine trying to navigated through the trees to the windows. It was noon when she finished. She went in to get warm, and fill her tummy with homemade soup. Soon, she napped.

Aching and stiff from the mornings work, Elizabeth was surprised to find it was already two o'clock when she woke. How much more could she do today? Stretching, she convinced herself there was enough time to do one more chore before it got dark. She went to gather her garden tools and gloves for digging up annuals. Elizabeth didn't like to cover her plants; she would rather save them the pain of a slow death by quickly removing them, then see them turn brown from the frost. Since it was getting ever closer to that time, she decided to do it today while it was still warm enough to work outside. There were four garden areas to deal with, one of which had two paths she would also have to clear of leaves later.

She worked diligently at her task, and one by one the mums, salvia, flowering cabbage, and other flowers were removed from the gardens. Finished, she sat to rest for a moment visualizing the many beautiful colors that would replace this barren ground next spring. Returning to the tractor Elizabeth got the snow fence and set it into place. Afterward, she drove the tractor and trailer back into the pole barn for the night.

She slowly walked back to the house and, once inside, built a fire. Elizabeth dressed in a pair of sweat pants, sweatshirt and slippers for the evening. Relaxed, with a cup of tea and *The Prairie Home Companion* after dinner, she was relieved three more things had been checked off her list.

# The Goose

I watched the single strands of clouds,

mares' tails,

passing high above the towering pine,

Norwegian pine.

I recalled the gaggle of geese plus one

Canada goose

that couldn't quite catch up.

I watched her tread air, reset her compass, and fly

North.


-Elizabeth Washburn

# Chapter 3

The Canada geese always flew over the 80 acre lake; it was a landmark on their route and a stopping point for many a gaggle, where many hours were spent after feeding in the farmers' fields. Sometimes there were three, four, or five gaggles gathered with their individual families, and it became quite a party! According to legend, after the glacial lakes were formed, they discovered they were all Canada geese and this was a good place for an annual reunion. When their reservations were up, as dictated by the point goose, onward south they flew.

One gaggle was already there when the second one came in. No one knows why the first had twenty geese and the second only twelve; that was just how it was. When the gaggle of twelve, probably two or three different families, landed, they sent up large sprays of water while simultaneously announcing themselves with a nasal quavering chant. Elizabeth called it goose music.

The geese always landed with their feet stretched forward and necks downward before setting down with a large spray; not unlike the smoke from the tires of a jet on a runway. Because these gaggles had had to fly into a strong wind, the geese landed with a whiffle, turning on their sides. Occasionally some of the younger geese would flip over completely, stall their air lift and plummet 5 or 10 feet before righting themselves. There were such antics that evening as three juvenile ganders flipped in the air. Then, on the horizon, one single goose appeared.

The goose was a magnificent bird dressed in the finest black and white collared neck feathers which reflected the sun as she came in for her landing. Because she was young her brown feathers had not become dulled through miles of flight. And even though she was somewhat smaller than her male counterparts, no one without a trained eye could tell them apart.

She had chosen to follow this particular gaggle when it was time to separate from her family. She was three; and all three year olds had been taught they were old enough to be on their own. She knew that she had no longer been welcomed and needed to fly at least one hundred miles from the nest of her mother and father.

She had a high pitched 'klink-klink ho-onk' voice rather than a males tenor 'ke-ronking ho-honk' one. She sang this song when she landed, while performing her own acrobatics. The goose landed well removed from the other two families so she could keep watch, lest they leave without her; she knew geese flew both day and night.

All the geese swam and preened and nibbled the tasty pond weeds, thoroughly enjoying themselves as if going to a ball or the opera. It was indeed a scene from *The Nutcracker,* as they imitated their cousins the swans. As they flew on this journey, they loved the Heartland rest. It had the best grains in the fields and always a lake near by at day's end, for attending to their "less-than-fit-for-a-proper-evening-out" geese selves. They especially loved this little lake because it was so quiet; hardly a human lived here all year except the crone, who was as much a part of nature as they were. During this period of gaiety, most of the geese did not notice the lone goose; but there was one exception, the 2 year old gander. Soon several young, mischievous males casually surrounded the goose. Her heart began to pump a little faster than normal and the goose was confused by their behavior. These young ganders had not learned their lesson. Geese were sociable; they should pride themselves on it, for so many other living things were not. They should have known, by watching their father, that the only time they shouldn't be courteous was during nesting. They outnumbered her 3 to 1 and her concern grew.

The ganders began posturing; like men with their chests puffed out, ready for a fight. Some had folded their necks while others had theirs protruding; all were pointed at her. They circled and circled, then all of a sudden started vertical head pumping, and a direct attack ensued as they opened their mouths and showed their teeth. Instinctively the goose folded her neck, pumped her head and fought back. Vigorous swinging of necks and rotating heads exemplified the violence with which they fought.

Then it stopped.

As the sky lost its last streaks of yellows and reds, turning the color

12

of a raven lit by tiny spotlights, a gander began tossing his head up and down making the long deep 'ho-onk' sounds indicating it was time to go. As if they had been working with a choreographer, a goose rose to lead the way with a gander guarding the rear. The all too familiar sound of goose music filled the air and the rest of the families left one after another on their journey. As the wedge was formed and headed south, the injured goose trailing behind decisively turned and headed north.

Elizabeth had been standing on her dock, listening to the uncommon commotion that had just ceased. She hadn't been able to find its source and barely saw the gaggles take off. "How much longer will fall last?" she whispered, her voice barely carrying across the water. Then, as she turned slowly away from the blue-black lake, she thought she saw a shadow on the lake.

# Chapter 4

As the light of day broke over the lake she floated as if dead. She was too tired to go in search of a farmer's field this morning. Although dubious of the gaggle that had just flown overhead, she knew instinctively the worst was over.

Her work for the day was simple enough, eat and nurse her wounds. Nicked gray spots had been randomly placed on her beautiful brown coat. The goose looked like a battle worn naval ship as she floated, ready to find her morning meal. She would land on shore occasionally, since there were still some nice green shoots of grass that the crone had provided, and then slowly drift away. On the far side, she was out of view of the crone's nest, and also found what she was looking for. It was shallow here and the vegetation grew thick and varied. There were tubers, roots, leaves, seeds, and algae near the bank. Submerging her head she chewed off these fine offerings, then lifted her head and swallowed water. Having had her fill, she found a nice protective hiding place among the grasses. Had she been able to be seen, one would have observed her getting out of the water, itching, and loafing. She did her loafing lying down; to stand today would be too much work. Soon she was so still, she looked asleep.

The goose made her trips to shore about every two hours throughout the day. Occasionally she would notice the crone on the shore, walking or riding on the back of a turtle. However, she didn't pay her much mind since she was more concerned about her needs and when her feathers might grow back. In the late afternoon, as the sky turned into the Painted Desert, the goose swam to Elizabeth's shore. Walking out of the water she proceeded to have her meal of unmowed, tender morsels of grass. When she finished she went back to the lake, preened, and looked as ready for the dance as she could look. She could hear gaggles fly by overhead and was happy they decided to land, preen, dance and move on with no incident tonight. As the light faded and she looked toward shore, she saw the crone's eyes shining warmly in the nest.

• • •

Wedges of geese continued to land in late afternoon and early evening. Although she kept her distance for over a week the goose became aware that the attack fifteen days ago had been a rare occurrence, and she was not afraid. Though still a bit cautious when the families began to dance *The Nutcracker,* she added her part. She had claimed her lake, which would be her nesting site next spring, and she was determined no other goose or gander would take it away.

# The Crone and The Goose

The crone and the goose were kindred spirits.

Both defied the logic of all snow birds.

They would spend *this* winter in the North.

-Elizabeth Washburn

Book 1

The
Winter

# Totem

Under stars of Capricorn

Renewal time;

Blowing in on north wind,

Elements, earth with air.


Birth and animal totem: goose.

Totem: buffalo.

Plant totem: bramble.

Mineral totem: peridot.

Polarity totem: woodpecker.

Affinity totem: white.


She is self-demanding,

Reliable, prudent, austere,

Ambitious, determined, preserving,

Rigid, pessimistic, demanding, selfish.

Conscious aim, conservation,

Subconscious desire, integrity.


Yin predominates.

-Elizabeth Washburn

# Chapter 1

"She seems to be exploring her life. I have seen this daily in my short time here on the lake. Although her body is aging her creative spirits soar. This is why the stories call her crone."

"I watch every movement she makes. I am her totem. I bring her messages about the seasons. I tell her, in her way, when fall and spring are coming. I am a good sign. Earlier in her life, when she was on the vision quest, I reminded her that she needed to get her life in order, become more organized, and be more cooperative. She has learned these lessons well. I also taught her the need for supporting one another and to assume the role of leadership when the existing leaders become too weak. She has now become a crone, a wisdom walking. She studies my behaviors to see how I plan and cooperate. A wise one still learns."

"From afar I see her ride on the back of a turtle, although a turtle shouldn't make sound. She creates a life for herself. I can tell because she seems happy with her chosen path."

"She builds, like my family built, a warm and cozy nest. Hers comes with smoke like her ancestors, the Mandan and the Lakota. The smoke comes from the wood she gathers from the earth. She never takes more than she needs. She *is* one with nature."

"I watch her watch the other birds and the deer, the bear, and the squirrels. She never harms them and she feeds them in their time of need. There is seed for the birds and salt for the deer, and corn cobs for the squirrels. The bear, the most powerful totem of all, will sleep soon; she will not feed it, it is not her totem, for hers will stay awake through the winter."

"She wears a goose on her collar to remind her of her first vision quest; the Goose Women, and those belonging to the Society of the White Buffalo Cow, used to perform the Goose Women rites to attract buffalo herds and ensure a plentiful corn harvest. I have seen that there is always plenty of corn in this part of the country. She uses it for her animals. These are as important to her and her relationship with the rest of the birds and animals as it was to the Mandan, the first tribe to settle in North Dakota. I could tell this vision quest became the most important occurrence in her life."

"As I now observe, the crone is in the North on her journey. Her qualities at this age are a compilation of the four directions. She is an elder, a mentor, a person in the web of life. This directional gift is balanced by the South; as do the East and West balance each other. The idealism of the South is balanced by the wisdom and clarity of thought learned in the North. That balance applied to the universal web becomes justice, the greatest gift of the North. The crone is 'Wisdom Walking'."

"She practices The Instructions Given by The Creator to Native People at The Time Of Creation:
- Take care of Mother Earth and all other colors of man.
- Respect Mother Earth and Creation.
- Honor all life and support that honor.
- Be grateful from the heart for all life. Through life there is survival. Thank the Creator at all times for all life.
- Love and express that love.
- Be humble. Humility is the gift of wisdom and understanding.
- Be kind with one's self and with others.
- Share feelings and personal concerns and commitments.
- Be honest with one's self and with others.
- Be responsible for these sacred instructions and share them with other nations."

· · ·

"I watched her going about her daily activities. She took turtle every day and rode on its back. One day she took the wood she had cut from the forest and put it in a pile closer to the lake. That same day she took shiny sheets and added them to her nest. She gathered the flowers in her wings and confined the ground which once held their beauty."

"When she was tired, like me, she would go to her nest. I never did see her drink the water from the lake and wondered if she ever got thirsty. Nor did she ever eat the grasses. I didn't know how she could exist this way."

"One day an elder, a sage, came by and they took something from the lake and put something back. What they put into the lake required them to float out. The object looked like a group of solid vines with a reed protruding from it. All of a sudden it started blowing water into the air. I was apprehensive so I stayed as far away as possible."

"Then they got a large turtle, the largest I have ever seen; it made the one the crone usually sat upon look like a gosling. It had four legs, two small ones on its front, two large ones on its back, both with round feet and it made lots of noise. The sage took its tail, hooked it to the long board in the water, got on the turtle's back and pulled the board out of the lake. That turtle struggled but it finally stopped when the sage got off and unhooked its tail."

"At day's end, as was her usual routine, the crone watched the geese land, and then take off for their night flight, always observing their behaviors. I never went with them. She exhibited the wisdom of a crone to let go of the geese so that new cycles may form. She is a transformer bringing unformed universe before us all."

# Chapter 2

Elizabeth's joints had stove up on her overnight from pulling the pump from the lake and putting the aerator in for the winter. She was not to be put off, though, by a little arthritic pain and was anxious to get back to work. So after her invigorating morning swim she was once again in good spirits and still capable of hard work. At least now, if that goose who was there every morning stayed, it would have fresh water to help it survive the winter. Then, as if grabbing for an imaginary point in the air in a high school geometry class, Elizabeth said to Carl's picture,

"I'm going to build a Canada Goose Nest Platform. This will give the goose protection from its predators and a warm place this winter, should it decide to stay longer."

Elizabeth drove her truck out of the pole barn and went the thirteen miles to town. Since she rarely did this, except to get groceries, she would have an adventure today.

Arriving at the lumber yard she purchased one 8 inch diameter, 12 foot long cedar pole and four 2 inch x 6 inch x 8 foot boards. She couldn't buy a washtub at the lumber yard and they suggested she go to the feed store. She purchased a 22 inch diameter round metal washtub there.

When Elizabeth got home she began work on the goose platform. First she cut the 12 foot cedar pole into three 4 foot lengths. She laid them on the ground 12 inches apart for a total length of 48 inches horizontally. Then she cut the boards into 4 foot lengths, laid them flat across the poles, forming a 48 inch square platform and nailed them in place. In the center of the platform she nailed the washtub. Lastly, she found two anchors and chains she used for her fishing boat.

Satisfied, she called her next door neighbor, Hal, and he came with his tractor to pull it down to the lake. Before they launched it they gathered straw, leaves, lake weeds and other such materials, from those bought and available on shore. The elders liked a nice, soft, warm, nest. Hal looked like Huckleberry Finn navigating the platform with a long pole as he brought it within the vicinity of the aerator. Elizabeth followed with a boat. The two, aerator and platform, were placed about 200 feet from shore. Hal wound the chains around a pole, fastened them with a lock and dropped the anchors into the water. Elizabeth expertly maneuvered the oars as Hal stepped his 200 pound frame into the unstable boat; his eyes were as big as saucers. Soon they were safely setting feet on dry land. Elizabeth was so pleased with herself that she couldn't wipe the grin from her face.

. . .

The sun continued on its appointed course as the earth rotated on its axis. The goose became very curious about the spouting water in the lake. She wasn't quite sure about the floating earth that had a big shiny nest in the middle of it either. But curiosity got the best of her and she began swimming closer and closer to the aerator, then back to the floating earth. Finally, she tentatively rose out of the water to walk on the very hard surface. She placed one foot in front of the other on this highly unfamiliar hard surface. It caused her much discomfort. She continued, though, as the round shiny hole was her ultimate destination. To the goose it looked much like the nest she had been brought up in. Flying into it, she discovered the vegetation in the metal tub. With the instincts of a mother goose she began tossing straw out. Although she had felt it before in the farmers' fields, it did not belong in a nest. Rearranging the other vegetation until the bedding felt just right, she was soon loafing. As the goose looked around though, something wasn't right. There were no reeds and grasses behind which she might hide and blend into. Panicked, she quickly flew across the lake. It wasn't a goose's nature to fly with material in her mouth, like her cousins, and it took many more trips than she had thought. Soon the material was stacked all around the inside of the tub and threatening to overflow. Laying back down, exhausted, the goose looked at peace.

She got up to eat, then back to rest, many times that day until she was used to the new shelter. She was very pleased with herself for adventuring into new territory. A goose usually is a creature of habit, but now she was forging her own way. Satisfied, she soon made preparations for the evening. There were many more gaggles than in previous evenings and there would be singing and dancing of grand proportions tonight. None of the other geese paid her much attention, as had been done not so long ago. Toward sunset some of the families proceeded on their way while a few decided to spend the night. The goose slept near her sanctuary just in case a predator might be lurking nearby.

• • •

Elizabeth watched from the comfort of her loft.

As dawn broke, Elizabeth was awake and ready to face the day. She went for her morning dip in the lake, which was now becoming a challenge as the temperatures dropped. The water was still about 45 degrees but the air temperature was only 38. She dried off and covered herself quickly. Maybe this was the year she would go from the spa to the snow and back in. Or maybe the sauna to the snow to the sauna would be her morning ritual. Either would be better than chopping holes in the ice, as she had done for the past ten years.

Dressing in her usual costume, without the outdoor garb, she began her day working on inside projects. She started with the spa. Procuring her cleaning fluids, made especially for the material from which the spa was made, she took off the top and cleaned its reverse side. She got into the spa without her shoes and cleaned it as well. Removing the side panel, which took all of her strength and lots of wiggling, she attached the hose to fill the tub. As the spa filled she read her book, Woodswoman by Anne LaBastille.

Elizabeth's life was that of a woods woman and she felt a kindred spirit of the author's. She had met Anne on a trip to the Adirondack wilderness in the late 70's, carrying her book in her backpack to be signed. In her journal Elizabeth had written:

Day 1

I met Anne at her remote wilderness cabin, on Black Bear Lake, after paddling in my canoe at some length. The cabin is fashioned, by her own hands, into a 12 foot by 12 foot room. It is more rustic than mine. We sat in the main room when I arrived, comfortable but sparse. She did have a porch but I guess today was not the day for that. For many hours we shared stories of our lakes, the life of the "woodswoman" and how being alone has affected our lives. As night fell, I set up my tent outside her cabin. The smell of the earth and the feel of the night eyes, the cries in the dark, are most dear to me.

Day 2

I helped Anne chop wood this morning for the fire on the shore. We took her boat out where we caught just enough to eat. I prepared a shore breakfast over the open fire. I got a tour of the wood shed and we sat on the sun deck where we both wrote. I enjoyed the silence and the companionship of another human being.

Later I told her about my heritage. I told her of my mother's struggle to leave her family when my father's expedition had worked their way onto the reservation. Even though we are different, we are the same.

Day 3

I asked Anne to sign my book, which she gladly did, before I left early this morning.

The trip back was long, and I must say I am glad to have a bed to lay on tonight.

. . .

When the spa had finished filling she got up, even though she wanted to remain with her friend, and returned the door, which was as hard to replace as it had been to remove; she locked it. Then turning the outside water off, and bringing the hose inside, she went upstairs for lunch. It was noon on the dot, just as Elizabeth liked it.

. . .

There were still many chores on Elizabeth's list. During lunch she had reviewed it with dismay as an unknown tiredness set in. Would she be ready for the first snowflake? It was possible in October, although it didn't usually stick. Gathering her shirt and such, she stepped into the afternoon air. It hadn't warmed much since the clouds had moved in early. The freshness hit her face like a slap. She was revived and moved quickly toward the pole barn.

Retrieving her tool box from under the work bench, Elizabeth walked over to her propped up Arctic Cats. She had two; one for herself and a 2-up for the company she was sure to have when the winter season was in full swing. She replaced the spark plugs with new ones, cleaned the air filters, checked the oil, and took the trickle chargers off the batteries. She sat on hers. Soon she was roaring across the ice of Lawson Lake. Mindful of the trail markers, she slowed to a steady pace. Joyful and invigorated, she then sat on the 2-up and drove leisurely down the pine lined trails winding through the woods, greeting oncoming snowmobilers with a raised mitten. Opening her eyes she shut the machine off.

Before completing her next two chores, Elizabeth sat on her motorcycle one last time for the season, dreaming about the days, not so long ago, when she'd had the pleasure of riding on country roads lined with cranberry, lemon, and banana-colored leaves. Her boat took her back one more season, and she wondered if the fishing this winter would be as good as it had been this summer. For now though, memories were all she had as she shimmied over the side of the boat, took the boat motor in her hand, and closed her eyes as she drove to her favorite fishing hole.

As Elizabeth finished she shivered, chilled by the gray sky. She decided to go inside to make a cup of hot cocoa. As she warmed, she braced herself to complete a couple more chores. It was now 3:00. She went to the *landing strip*, as she called the large strip of land facing the lake. Slowly mounting the John Deere, she began taking up the leaves in the leaf attachment. It took about an hour and a half and darkness was falling quickly. She'd had to bag them and dump them in the compost pile, which she could barely see in the failing light. The comforting hoot of a nearby owl accompanied her as she finished.

She was shivering more profusely when she went inside, and built a fire as quickly as possible. The flames through the grill visually warmed her body, even before she felt the heat. Sitting down in her favorite chair with a Snowshoe Grog, Elizabeth let her internal temperature rise to that of the outside flames. Elizabeth looked fondly at the man in the picture as if he were there. She quietly whispered, as if into his ear, "A dinner of hearty chicken pot pie is in order tonight."

• • •

As predicted on the radio last night, the new day brought slightly warmer temperatures in the 50's. She still needed her wool shirt and long underwear, winter muffs to keep her ears warm and, of course, her lined leather work gloves in the morning. After dressing and unlocking the pole barn, Elizabeth began maintenance on the John Deere. She lay down on the cold concrete floor to change the oil. The cold seemed to seep through her many layers of clothing. Removing her gloves, her fingers rapidly turned to ice. Then standing, she changed the plugs. The task of taking off the mowing deck found her once again on the cold floor. She managed to finish in about 40 minutes and decided a spa would be in order tonight. Removal of the leaf attachment was effortless, but the snow blower was laborious to put on. The latter two took a little over two hours.

Once again having lunch and getting warmed up, but with no nap, she was ready to get back to work. This time she began with raking the leaves in the back yard. The crunch made her feel like a kid again and as the piles grew she couldn't help herself; she had to jump into one, even though it meant raking it up again. When the piles were considerable in size she put them into 30 gallon plastic bags and carried each one to the drain field. This was repeated 12 times. The sun had warmed the air and by now she was working in only a light shirt, though still long sleeved. The remainder of the leaves were raked into the driveway and burned after 4 p.m. A county-issued a permit would not let you burn any sooner because the danger of fire was greater before 4 p.m. due to wind conditions. All of the intense labor Elizabeth had gone through that day was beginning to take its toll. She knew however, that if she stopped now the leaves would never get burned today, and the weather was always unpredictable, no matter what the good looking meteorologist said.

After lighting the nine piles of leaves and twigs, as well as a pile in the fire pit, it was a little past 7:00 before they had burned low enough that she could go inside. She returned from indoors, her arms full with dinner preparations. As she sat on a log, waiting for the coals to be just the right temperature for cooking, she stared through the trees at the sky and remembered all the animals, the birds, the geese, and the lone goose, and wondered if they were completing their chores before winter. She always felt such a kinship to them in the fall, as if the spirit planned things that way. Soon she was cooking beans in the cast iron kettle, a brat on a stick, and drinking a beer. Even though the moon shone brightly, the infinite dome of stars accompanied Elizabeth as she continued to eat her food and sip her beer. Elizabeth marveled at the sparks shooting into the atmosphere from the fire. Then, as the night time animals of the forest began their songs, the fire died and the night chill began working on her bones; Elizabeth reluctantly conceded it was time to go in.

# Chapter 3

Elizabeth had been soaking and enjoying the first view of winter from her spa when, beyond all reason, she dashed spontaneously into the cold morning air. It was at that point she noticed the goose swimming near the aerator and envied the bravery of her totem. Cold icy fingers had walked the lake last night leaving a thin layer of frozen water.

Elizabeth was glad she had dug her flowers up early this year. The past five nights, the temperature had been in the 20 degree range. Any flowers left would have been dead from frost in the morning, even if they had been covered. She knew the goose could still find food that morning, since vegetation rose above the ice, and upon flying to the farmers' fields there would still be much stubble and corn to be had. As the day progressed, the ice would be gone and the grass frost free. She knew the goose had nothing to worry about today.

· · ·

The weeks passed quickly leading up to Thanksgiving. The nights became more frigid, until the lake finally froze up, as the cold icy fingers had shattered into thousands of cracked fragments, which had spread and frozen with each blast of breath from the wind. The last of the geese were passing by, looking for an open body of water. Elizabeth was having Thanksgiving dinner for all her friends within the vicinity: permanent north country residents; friends from as far back as she could remember. Only Elizabeth and Hal and Gwen were permanent residents on Snowshoe Lake; or, as one of her ancestors had named it, "Walking on Lake". As she was stuffing the turkey, her mind wandered back to the first month she had lived there, and to meeting Hal, her closest friend and neighbor.

"Nice day out there," said the man sitting next to her at the counter.

"A bit cold," Elizabeth had replied.

"I seen some of the lakes iced over last night. Going to be a long cold winter."

"I saw the northern lights about midnight last night." Elizabeth had quickly picked up his lack of sophistication and did not use the term *aurora borealis*.

"Too late for me. So, do you live 'round here?"

"Yes, over on Snowshoe Lake. I just moved here from the cities," she said, warming up to him. She had seen him before but never paid much attention. Carl had been her whole life before she moved here permanently ten years ago. They only used their place on the weekends before that, and had the lake to themselves.

"I heard you was a teacher?"

"Well, I'm not exactly now. My husband and I used to come up on the weekends when he was alive, but we pretty much kept to ourselves. We had our place, where I now live, on the end of a private road. I was a teacher then, but now that I am retired and have moved up here, I need to become somewhat less of a hermit. I am a writer. I haven't even met my neighbors yet. What do you do?"

"You know Ted Wright?"

"No."

"Well, him and I have this operation where we haul dirt and rock. In the winter we plows others' drives."

"Hmm, I have been looking for someone to plow my road now that I'll be living here year round. What's your name?"

"Hal, short for Henry."

"Hal? That's my neighbor's name also, but I haven't met him yet. He lives in the old Mickerson's place about three quarters of a mile up the road on the way to mine."

"That's me," said Hal with a slight grin. "Gwen and I've been meaning to walk down to meet you. She'll bring some bars when we come."

"Would you be willing to plow as far down as the turn around? I can, and want to, do the rest of the road down to the lake."

"Seeming as I already plow to my place I don't sees why not."

"You want a warm up Hal?"

"Sure, and give, what's your name?"

"Elizabeth."

"Sure, and give Elizabeth here one, too."

. . .

Turkey stuffed, she put it into the oven. It would take over six hours to cook; a good thing she got up at 5 this morning.

Elizabeth turned her attention to the Cranberry Orchard Salad. Without this dish, her guests would go away disappointed. Most of the women and a couple of the men had asked her for the recipe at one time or another. The directions were easy though.

Cranberry Orchard Salad

1 six ounce package of orange Jell-O

16 ounce package of cranberries chopped

1 orange diced

1/2 cup of sugar

1/8 teaspoon of cloves

1/4 teaspoon cinnamon

1/4 teaspoon salt

2 cups of boiling water

1 1/2 cups cold water

1 tablespoon lemon juice

8 ounce package of walnut pieces

Mix berries and sugar together-set aside

Dissolve Jell-O and salt in boiling water

Add cold water, lemon juice, cinnamon, and cloves

Place in refrigerator till Jell-O is thickened but not firm

Fold in the rest of the ingredients and let stand in refrigerator until firm.

May take longer if using a plastic bowl. Serves 6.

Elizabeth always doubled it, so if there were leftovers, and if someone wanted to, they could take them home.

She checked on the turkey about every two hours.

. . .

Her house would be full today. Hal and Gwen, of course, Della and her son John, Suzy and her boyfriend Ken, Della's two daughters,

Carol and Judy and the two boys, and Ted. Counting herself, that made twelve.

There would be beer, or wine if they preferred, and pop for the children or anyone else that might not want to drink alcohol. After dinner, of course, there would be sherry, pumpkin pie, apple pie, ice cream, and coffee. Laughing to herself, she thought about the figurines she always put on top of the pumpkin pie. There was an Indian crouched behind brush, bow and arrow aimed at a wild turkey. Of course it was meant to be a spoof, but the men always took it so seriously. They would debate the truth of the myth, until they finally gave in to Elizabeth's expertise.

Focusing on the tasks at hand once more, Elizabeth went over her list: mash potatoes, cool winter squash, fix green bean salad, tossed salad later. She would start the potatoes about 45 minutes before the turkey was done so she would have time to mash them while the turkey set. The salads would be ready to go, and when the turkey came out and was setting, the pies would go in. Her totem had taught her well in the organization department.

. . .

Soon her company started arriving. She had seating for twelve in her crowed living room by borrowing the chairs from the dining room. The younger people sat on pillows on the floor at first, when they all began to gather. Soon drinks and appetizers had been placed on the coffee and end tables. There were crackers and cheese, olives, potato chips, dips, and spreads. Each person warned another not to eat too much, so they would have room for dinner and dessert.

Then, just like clock work, the meal was placed on the tables; both dining and card table. The women helped, as the tables had already been set earlier by Elizabeth.

Hal said grace and Ted carved the turkey. Soon everyone was eating with much delight. Accolades were given for another delicious Thanksgiving meal.

After dinner and before dessert, the games started. Some were playing Sequence, others President, while still others got into Spades. There was much laughter and fun until Ben, one of Della's grandsons, in one swoop, cleared the card table because he was always the Hole in President. His brother, of course, seemed to always be President. It was time for pie, ice cream, coffee and/or sherry to calm the embattled nerves. About 10:00, everyone went home; happy and content, having spent a day with friends.

# Chapter 4

The first snow came a little over two weeks later. Twenty inches fell over the course of a day and a half. It matched the largest amount ever recorded. Since the temperatures were predicted to stay in the low 30's for a least the next two weeks, it didn't look like it would melt before spring. Many of the fish in the lake would probably die this winter giving the eagles quite a banquet come spring.

Schools were closed. The residents on Snowshoe Lake were snowed in. It was too fluffy even to snowmobile. All they would do is sink and get stuck. The only things moving were the snowplows, the snowmobile trail groomers, and, once they had their drives plowed out, the four-wheel drive SUV's.

When the goose woke for her morning feeding there was not a blade of grass or any lake vegetation to be seen, but since she spent the night in the open water, she was able to drink and find vegetation to feed on when diving. The snow had weighted down her wings. The platform was covered with layers and layers of snow. She was able to flap her wings to remove the snow but there seemed no way to walk to the nest which was filled in also. The cold began to penetrate.

She closed her eyes. Looking into her dreams, she sought a solution. As a totem, she brought many things to the people she looked after. This was the time coming of the people that had been born in winter. The sacred circle was in the North of the Four Directions. It was up to her to look to how she too, as her people did, would survive in this web of the universe. Separating from her fears, the goose began thinking more clearly now.

Returning to the center of the Medicine Wheel, she saw how she fit together with everything else. She would take action from that Balance Point because it was good to do so. She had flapped her wings to blow the snow away, but she couldn't fly to her nest for lack of enough running room. She tried placing one foot forward, then the other. She started to sink in the white fluffy stuff as she ventured out of the water. As the goose went further and further into the snow, she sunk deeper and deeper until she was up to her belly. Her fear took over and she was no longer free. She stopped. Three of the gifts of the North were to think, remember, and solve problems. Thinking she could not be afraid, she stopped struggling and tried to remember what other means of movement she possessed.

The goose started moving her legs and feet, as if swimming, a little at a time. After about twenty minutes, she was tiring and ready to stop when she felt something familiar. It was the ground, or more specifically the ice. She was about a foot from the edge of the water but, with the determination to finish what she began, she kept moving her feet. She had about fifteen yards to go from the water to the edge of the platform. At this rate it would take her another five or six hours to finish. She dreamed of the days when she had first swum for hours, never lacking in the desire for adventure. She would look at this struggle as an adventure, and swim for hours if needed. When the goose became hungry and thirsty, she would walk back and forth managing to have an evening meal, though meager. Throughout her ordeal that night, the image of the Great Mountain was in front of her, reminding her that the higher she climbed, the steeper and more difficult the way became. Yet the higher she went, the more she could see, and the stronger she would become. When she got to her nest, the goose swam and flapped her wings even harder until most of the snow had disappeared.

Day after day, twice a day thereafter, the goose would make her journey back and forth from the nest to the water, to keep a path clear. She was getting thinner and thinner as the days wore on. Although she had plenty of fat and could find some vegetation under the water, it was not enough to sustain her. She began to speculate on what would happen if she continued to stay here for the winter.

One morning after her walk back to the nest, she noticed activity near the nest on the hill. The crone was on the back of her turtle with a large mouth protruding from its head. Its mouth was so large that it ate all the white in its path. She wondered how the Spirits of the North would like that. Down the hill, closer and closer she got to the goose. Then she stopped the turtle, turned, and headed back. That was the closest they had ever been. Not knowing what the crone might do next, she hid in her nest.

Sure enough, another animal, like a caterpillar, came roaring toward her with the crone on its back. The goose tried to detach herself from her fear, but nestled further and further down in her nest. As she peeked, she noticed the white becoming a path right under its feet; a path with little caterpillar tracks in it. The crone rode it a safe distance from the water's edge, then continued around the lake. She often came close to the areas on the shore that the goose had discovered were good places to eat and stopped. Then back she went, and the goose couldn't believe her eyes. The wing of the crone was throwing yellow beads all over the path, from near the platform to the shore. When all the paths were covered with the beads up on land, she went back to the caterpillar's hole.

Cautiously the goose got out of her nest and inspected the path. To her great delight, the crone's yellow beads were actually corn from the farmers' fields. Although she had flown to fields after the white came, she had seen nothing but more white there and wondered where the corn had come from. She didn't care, however, because the corn was here.

Elizabeth watched from her cozy home.

· · ·

The goose grew accustomed to the crone's daily visits on the caterpillar. By goose time, it seemed as if there was a constant supply of corn, yet Elizabeth only distributed it every third day. The goose ventured further from the safety of the platform every day as she discovered corn wherever the caterpillar went. One day she discovered, at the end of a path, a familiar place. She began honking with great joy; this had been where she had nursed her wounds so long ago. To her great goose delight, there was still the stubble of that long ago green vegetation. She enjoyed a treat that day.

Everyday the goose would wake from her night in the bubbling water and end the day there. She always saw the beautiful sunrises' glancing rays of light bouncing off the white, and when there weren't clouds, the deep blue sunsets. If she was up late enough, with just the right conditions, sometimes thousands of dancing lights could be seen in the sky. They reminded her of a long lost spiritual place one of her ancestors had been to, and told about through the stories. They said, one by one the lights would come out of hiding and sometimes make pretty pictures in the sky. The goose barely had a language for expressing how these made her feel. When the shadows cast indigo paths interspersed with the bright white, and the long lanky fingers protruded from the trees, the goose would go for a stroll. About the only beast she ran into, although she always kept a mindful watch for predators, was an occasional deer who had not bedded down for the night. She would hear the cry of a lonely, hunting owl, and was thankful for the company.

One dancing light night, after her evening meal and preening time, she stayed up for an improvised ball. The middle of the lake was her stage with a checkerboard floor of indigo and white. As if she'd had lessons in ballet, the goose began moving her wings, her feet, and stepped to the undulating music of the sky. All at once she began singing her distinctive song, the notes originating from deep within her soul. The lamplight yellows and cold blues of the sky danced in the three part play. "Ho-onk, ho-onk, ho-onk..." resonated through the Wisconsin forest that night. Its echoes could be heard as far away as the county road. Those people still up, wondered at a goose making music so late into the season. Every person, every animal, and every owl began singing their own music and the Spirit of the North was pleased.

# Chapter 5

It had taken a few days before Hal could plow her out. He had worked on the areas that were vital first, like the parking lots at the medical clinic and the fire station. He also belonged to the local snowmobile club and helped groom the hundreds of trails in Wyngate County. When a snowfall of this magnitude came, the snowmobilers were very impatient to ride; the trails had to be opened as soon as possible; this was a vital to the economy of the area.

In the meantime, the snow flew up and around the cab of Elizabeth's snowblower like 'cotton' from the cottonwood trees. Once, her friend Sarah, had taken a picture of this happening through the sunlight, towards the house. In the picture, which she had framed as a gift, it looked like white lights on a Christmas tree without your glasses on or through a fog; it depended on your perspective.

Snowfall, A Poem

First snow has all but stopped,

but the green and white,

bright white,

remains.

       The first snow of the season came

       in a friendly way,

       descending throughout the quiet hours of night.

The first began late last night.


Looking out the window

from the second story bedroom

she awoke,

with delight.

       First snow has all but stopped,

       but the green and white,

       bright white,

       remains.

-Elizabeth Washburn

. . .

The snow fall was so deep Elizabeth plowed two more days. She had to plow it three times to make the road wide enough for her truck to turn around below. Then, as luck would have it, just as she was beginning to get cabin fever, Hal and the big plow came in the following day.

Throughout the ordeal, Elizabeth had observed the goose's struggle and decided she needed help bringing balance to her life. Yes, the goose was making her way; she could hardly believe the path it had made in the snow as the ice became thicker. She also knew the vegetation in the area of the aerator was scarce and it wouldn't be long before the goose would be too weak to search for it. If that goose was determined to stay the winter, then she would continue to help it eat as she always helped the rest of the birds and animals.

Thanks to Hal, she headed into town the next day with a list a mile long. Elizabeth rejoiced in the beauty that was all around her. Her trip was unusually long as she had to stop to talk to all her friends. Hal was gone but Gwen was there and invited her for lunch on her way back. Della, who could talk faster than a politician campaigning, was next. No sooner had Elizabeth entered Della's home than out came a cup of coffee; the worse cup of coffee in the county. She barely had time to take off her coat before the conversation started.

"I been wondering how yous was doing-that was quite a storm. Most of the county lost power for two days. Did yous lose power? I was worrying about yous, but then Hal stopped in and said yous had not had any problem with the 'lectric."

"Yes, it was quite a storm," answered Elizabeth, knowing that anything longer than a short reply would just be futile.

"John couldn't get into work for a day. Thankful the roads was cleared day after. You know he doesn't get paid if he misses. I wouldn't like being down wheres yous live on my own. Lord have mercy! How did yous survive anyways?"

As Della took a breath Elizabeth took the opportunity to talk. "Well, I used my snowblower and plowed around the house to bide my time. I knew it would be a few days before I was plowed out. I also watched my goose and I am on my way to town to get it some corn to eat now."

"Goose, what goose?" Della asked, ready to listen this time.

"Well, this goose came to visit in early fall, sometime before Halloween I think. Anyhow, I looked into the sky, just about dark one evening, when I saw this goose turn away from the rest of the flock and fly north. Next morning, wouldn't you know, it was on my lake and it has never left," Elizabeth said, using flock instead of gaggle to keep the vocabulary simple.

"What a silly goose," Della said, laughing at her joke. "Did you know John hunts geese? He says they are no good as they are all over the fields. He says they all should be shot or cart away. He says only a dead goose is a good goose. Doesn't that get your gander? Ha!"

"I've got to go, Della, but you should get John to bring you down for lunch on Sunday after church, and see the goose with your own eyes." Elizabeth had finished her cup of coffee and wasn't about to have a third one since Della had taken a pause and was bound to see her cup was empty.

"Sorry to see you go, our visit just got started. We will come though."

Elizabeth got in her truck, waved good-bye, and headed on down the washboard, snow-packed road.

She drove slowly since the sand, sprayed in the middle of the road, barely graced the right or left lane. "What a beautiful day," she exclaimed to the sun and the trees, the land and the animals, "What a beautiful day!" Breaking out in song, *Oh What a Beautiful Morning*, Elizabeth drove on. As she neared the top of Blake Hill she had to swerve as a car, hugging the middle, shot over the top. Elizabeth became a bit annoyed at the break in her otherwise glorious drive. Soon, however, she finished her song.

Her first stop was the feed store.

"So what kind of animal you feeding now? Or maybe you need another metal tub? I got you a couple of salt blocks 'cause I knew you would be coming by sooner or later but I also know you, and you always have something else on your mind. Do you need bird seed; I'd of thought you had enough for the winter?" Jake must have been feeling the lack of customers in the days since the storm; this was a lot of talking for him.

"Thanks for putting the blocks aside. I do have enough seed for the snowbirds but I also need some shelled corn. I have this goose that has decided to winter on my lake and this storm was quite rough on her finding enough to eat."

"You don't say. A goose in the winter? This far north has to be a first. How much corn do you want?"

"I had better get 100 pounds for now. I really don't know how much it will eat, but any leftovers the deer will love to nibble on."

"I'll load it in your truck."

"Thanks. What do I owe you?"

"I'll make it 15.50 for you as you're always doing something for the wildlife around here."

" I'll be seeing you Jake."

After that she drove to the grocery store and chatted with a few of her friends from church whom she happened to run into there. They mostly talked about the snow and that they would see each other at Sunday mass.

Climbing back into the driver's seat and turning on the radio, she went home; singing along with her favorite country tunes. Elizabeth kept her coat on as she put away her groceries. When she finished she put on her gaiters over her pants and boot tops, went outside and strapped on her snowshoes. The shoes made a hollow sound as she went tromping through the woods, on the path to Gwen's house. It was shorter and far less hilly than going by the road.

Gwen had made a crock pot full of hearty ham and split pea soup. The place smelled warm and cozy and Elizabeth saw she had just taken fresh homemade bread from the oven. She could taste the creamy textured real butter on the bread and the hot steamy bowl of thick pea soup. It made her stomach talk.

"Hang your coat on the rack, take your boots off, and go warm your toes by the fire," Gwen said, warm and friendly.

"Thanks, I will. This is the first time I've been snowshoeing this winter and I worked up quite a sweat. I don't want to catch a chill."

As Elizabeth was warming her hands and feet, Gwen went about setting the table and cooling the bread so it could be cut.

"Would you like a cup of tea, cocoa, coffee...?"

"Well, I had my fair share of coffee at Della's this morning but herbal tea sounds just great. Do you have Mood tea?" Elizabeth asked knowing that Gwen always kept it on hand.

"Yes, coming right up. You just sit back and get nice and toasty warm."

"Have you and Hal been snowmobiling yet? I bet the trails are just beautiful."

"Not yet. Hal hasn't had time, but we were thinking of going out Thursday; would you like to join us?"

"Oh yes! I have been dying to go. As soon as the first flake fell I wanted to ride, but of course I would never go by myself, too big a risk. You know my sense of direction!"

"Well then, it's a done deal."

Tea in hand now, Elizabeth's mind began to wander. Life was like a lattice. We all live together and we know each other in so many different ways. She was so happy she could almost burst.

Gwen interrupted her thoughts. "Elizabeth, Elizabeth did you hear a thing I was saying? Or have you wandered off to that place I just don't understand?"

"Sorry. I was feeling so warm and cozy I took a mind break. So, what did you say?"

"It's time to eat."

"Okay! You don't have to call me twice," she laughed.

During lunch the two close friends had one of their affectionate talks. Gwen talked about her grandchildren and all their wonderful accomplishments. Of course that suited Elizabeth just fine; she never tired of talking about education. Elizabeth talked about the goose, the observations she had made of her, and the chapbook she was writing. They laughed about Della's coffee. They spoke fondly of riding through bent, bough-laden pines on their snowmobiles.

Finally, after saying her good-byes, Elizabeth went snowshoeing back through the forest knowing nothing defines who she is but her love for herself, and by that love and her friends she was defined.

Taking time for a bathroom break and to warm up, it wasn't long before Elizabeth was ready to go out again. This time she looked like a multi-colored snowman as she dressed in her snowmobile bibs, insulated boots, snowmobile jacket, gloves, and grabbed her helmet. All that talk about going trail riding on Thursday had gotten the juices running and she just had to take her sled out. Besides, Gwen would hear her and check from time to time while she was on the lake. And that goose did need to be fed. She went out to the pole barn, took the sled off the stand,

and started it up. It turned over easily and made the put put, soothing, loud, sound of a sled just tuned. She drove it out the pole barn door.

Elizabeth rode it around the turn around to just get the hang of it. Then she took off for her first official ride; she picked up her mail. When she got back she headed for the lake. Over the last week it had had time to freeze four inches because it was a shallow lake. That was enough for a snowmobile to cross on, even with the heavy snow. People who don't know about living in the north get the chills thinking about walking, snowmobiling, or driving on a lake. "How could it freeze so deeply that it would support that kind of weight?" Elizabeth's friends living in Missouri would ask. Why, they would not even walk on the ice, much less ride, even after seeing her do it.

She wanted to see how the aerator was doing. So she drove out near the platform and as close as she could to the water. She didn't want to get as close as a summer neighbor, who had come up for a lark one winter without telling anyone, had gotten a little too close to the one on the other side of the lake, and fell in. Fortunately Hal had seen him and went to his rescue. All Elizabeth could do was grab a shop broom and run across the lake to help. What she would have done when she got there she had obviously not thought through.

Returning to the pole barn she broke open the bag of corn and scooped out a five pound pail worth. She was about to have an adventure. She rode out and across the lake, going from island to island, shore to shore, north, west, south and east and every direction in-between, until the lake looked like a crossword puzzle. She made sure that every trail ended near some protruding vegetation.

She could hear the ice crackle, from the cold and the waves made by the weight of her snowmobile. Her ears hurt it was so silent in the wonderland. As she listened to the ice, she would clear areas of grasses with her shovel, a shovel that folded for convenience.

Wisdom Walking was determined to help the goose come into balance with nature once more. She distributed corn on the paths, around the platform, and up to shore. The goose watched.

# Chapter 6

Elizabeth had been very busy the past two weeks. Christmas was her favorite time of the year. Her birthday was the 24th so she not only celebrated the Christian's Jesus' Birthday with him, she got to celebrate her gifts from the totem and the gifts of the North. She was particularly joyous this year because her totem had come to her and shown herself.

Elizabeth returned early from her annual shopping for baskets and ribbons and crinkly wrapping paper. She also had bags of dried and fresh fruits, nuts, and teas. As she put aside her purchases Elizabeth began to fill her kitchen with the sweet odors of chocolate, walnuts, peaches, and cherries, and oh...so many cheerful, sweet, smells. She made homemade candy, small fruitcakes, and breads of all sorts over the course of a week. Her only outside activity was her goose run on the lake. The week before Christmas she put her baskets together. Every basket contained fruit and nuts and a favorite tea. Some baskets even had hot cocoa if the recipient had children. Each basket was personalized with a different candy, sometimes peanut brittle, sometimes assorted chocolates. Each contained a fruit cake, and some bread as well. Once each item had been meticulously placed, the wrapping was added. Her baskets looked professionally done. She twisted the paper at the top just so and added a beautiful ribbon without disturbing the wrapping. Every basket had a different color ribbon, depending on its contents, so she would know where the basket was to be delivered. Her biggest joy came on Christmas day when she would drive around on her snowmobile, pulling a little red wagon filled with baskets, delivering them to all her friends. It was the one day she did go out riding by herself because everyone knew she was coming and would go looking if she were late, just like Santa Claus.

. . .

One cold night, Elizabeth took to the woods with her chain saw, just like a lumberjack. She had told Hal she was going to cut a Christmas tree and should be back in an hour. She would call when she returned and if she didn't he should come looking for her. She told him about where she would be. Elizabeth never cut with the chain saw without someone knowing.

The full moon's light descending through the naked trees made it as bright as day as the beams reflected off the snow. It seemed as if someone had put luminaries on the paths in the woods. Elizabeth had put on her snowshoes to make the going easier. She had a good idea of where she would get her tree since she had seen it, in late fall, on a hike down the trail. It was about five feet high, or would be when cut down. It took her about 15 minutes to find it and another twenty to get the underlying branches cut off. She placed these in a circular path knowing it would make a warm spot for a deer to bed down.

Elizabeth tied a rope around the bottom branches that were left and the other end around her waist. Before moving it, though, she raised her eyes and her hands to Grandfather sky and thanked him for giving life to celebrate this joyous season. She also thanked Grandmother for the earth from which the tree grew. Then she thanked the tree for its life, turned and headed home.

Elizabeth anchored the tree in a pail of water. Every decoration would be used. She had no more; nor less, than the tree could hold no matter its size. She put on the green lights, green because they reflected the ornaments but did not distract from the beauty of the tree. Then meticulously she hung the ornaments on the tree. The birds always went closer towards the top while the larger animals went in between. Around and around the tree Elizabeth walked placing the forest animals. The whole tree was filled with the birds and animals of the forest, save one. That was a Santa ornament she had had since a child and it always got the place of honor; front and center, flanked by a family of bears, the greatest of all totems. To finish adorning the tree, she hung real tinsel strand by strand until the tree glistened with or without lights. Then finally she topped it with a goose.

Tired out and feeling a little blue, Elizabeth sat and read the many birthday and Christmas cards from her friends. She especially enjoyed the ones from Arizona. There were pictures of cacti, mountains and flowering shrubs so different yet containing as much life as the forests of the north. Then there were the pictures of her friends in the desert by their jeeps, or at home by their casitas. All of them came with a funny message like "have a prickly pear for your birthday." That one showed a woman sitting in front of a prickly pear cactus with her right hand raising a drink to a saguaro saying, "Here's to you old gal. May you live a good long life."

Her favorite Christmas card this year was a scene of the nativity sent by a student she'd had in her third year of teaching. There were many wise men, not just three, following the Biblical account, and there were animals of all different kinds. The barn where Mary and Joseph were was in the center of a village with many activities surrounding it. There was the market with fresh fruits and breads, the blacksmith shop, the sheep herders, and a stream nearby. Looking at this made her introspective and contemplative, but no longer blue.

Elizabeth had lit fire and was having a Snow Shoe Grog when she heard a voice singing in the night air. Looking up, as she had lost all track of time, she saw one of the reasons why she wintered here and didn't go south. Through the trapezoid windows was an undulating night sky, filled with blues and yellows and greens. The Aurora Borealis. The voice rang out with each wave of lights dancing in the sky. She recognized it as the voice of a goose. It must be bringing peace and joy to the people born during this season. Then Elizabeth found herself singing in tune, an old chant learned from her ancestors. She floated around the room, caught in the moment of the night spirits' song, not realizing the goose was dancing along.

# Chapter 7

As January made its move into the calendar year plunging the ladies deeper into winter, the goose was still living a quiet, peaceful life. She had come to like the winter and had actually grown more down to take care of the cold around her. Today did not seem like one of those days when it would be extraordinarily cold though, even with white on the horizon, because the clouds seemed light years away. However, they moved in silently while the goose was going about feeding, unexpectedly drowning out the sunlight, and began to shed their dandruff on the earth below.

The goose did not fear the white, driving and blowing in from the sky, but actually liked seeing it fall and melt when it hit the water near her nest. It was great to be a goose in the north on a day like today. She continued feeding, knowing that the white that fell from the sky would cover up the corn if she didn't get all her feed soon. The crone usually didn't bring more until the white stopped falling and she disliked trying to find it underneath. So preoccupied was she in her enjoyment of the snow and food that she failed to see what was really happening. She had no sense of 'winter snow' time.

As she made her way lazily around the path, the blowing wind took over this peaceful balance she had with nature, and she finally went back to her nest for protection. There was already half an inch in the nest that had to be cleared. She worked quickly and then decided to loaf before her evening meal. The white began to drift over her and she kept having to shake it off. The loafing became a lost cause. This was an all day job and began to tire her by nightfall. Now evening, it was time to feed one last time. She decided to fly to the island that still had much vegetation on it; the corn was now covered over with white here. Taking off into the wind was a difficult, blinding experience. The blowing pelted stuff into her eyes and took her breath away. Hunger, however, won the battle.

Her landing was less than perfect as she tipped on her side and almost flipped over. It was still very odd to land on the white this way but she had adapted well. What she found was of much concern. The stubble had been drifted over and no food could be seen. The paths were covered over and the vegetation beneath the opening in the water was slim pickings. She decided flying back was not an option. It would take too much energy. So she melted an area in the whitened ground to spend the night, fearful she could not get back.

When Elizabeth went to bed she had no idea what was happening to the goose.

Disoriented upon wakening, she wondered how she got here. Then the goose remembered the storm and heading to one of the islands in search of food. As she looked around she knew she had found one where the vegetation was thick. Continuing to turn her head, however, produced none in sight. As she looked around she realized she was better protected here than on that platform, even though there was no water nearby, and realized why she had stayed the night. Knowing she could get by with the little vegetation left below the water, and that she needed to drink, she tried to move. She was stuck. Not having eaten or drank in eight hours, she found herself in quite a predicament. She centered herself, before the fear could take over. Once calmed and warmed by the sun, the white would melt underneath her body: if she just waited.

She looked across the expanse of white and could see the crone taking the white stuff off her platform by trying to gather it with a small mouth hanging off her wing. She wondered why she didn't use her wings to blow it around. Maybe once the crone had finished her own nest she would get on the caterpillar's back and find her. She had grown less shy of the crone due to the corn she provided.

The sun now stood as high in the sky as it would all day. Her feathers loosened up, but as she tried to stand on her feet her legs gave out. She tried to fluff out her wings to move the snow underneath her and closer to the ground. She hoped she could get to some food as her body was beginning to shut down. The white stuff wouldn't move. Then she thought if she could just get off the ground she could fly to her other nest, but that didn't work either. She was permanently stuck. With hope she watched the crone on the big turtle with the wide mouth, eating up the snow. As the crone approached the edge of the land and rode the caterpillar down the hill she stopped. Noticing the sky filling with yellows and reds, it was at that precise moment the goose knew she would not be rescued tonight, for the caterpillar turned and headed for its hole. The goose wondered if she could make it without water one more night.

The sky turned dark, the moon cast its shadows, the stars made their pictures, the cold froze the white once again around her wings, and the goose sank further into her jail.

# Chapter 8

New Years Day dawned bright and sunny as Elizabeth prepared to celebrate the crones' ceremony. She scanned her table to be sure everything was in its place. This was the first ritual of the year that a crone performed. A crone travels through the seasons; the first is the illuminating season. The loft was the ideal location for the rituals. The ritual of the New Year coincided with the teachings of the Medicine Wheel that Elizabeth learned from her mother. In the loft there were curtains to draw and an environment free of most furniture, save a table, a rocking chair, and a day bed. There was much space in which to be illuminated. The flight of Earth about Sun carried life into the universe again. The light stands to reenact the eternal cycle. On the table were laid many items to believe in the unseen. Here Elizabeth would be taught many lessons about a new day coming.

At sunrise the ceremony began. A candle was lit behind a mortar full of pure white chalk, ground to dust. Elizabeth said to the sun, "I am the light of all days that are passed and my name is Preparation." Then she lit a candle behind a bowl of ice as she said, "I am the light of the day, today, and my name is Renewal." Then she lit a candle behind a prism and recited, "I am the light of all days to be, and my name is Revelation." Elizabeth followed these important words, Preparation, Renewal, and Revelation, with many explanations of January of the new year.

After the ceremony Elizabeth saw what daylight had also brought, snow drifting due to a 40 mile per hour wind. The cold snap, always accompanied by clear cold nights, wouldn't be over for a few days. The jet stream would have to shift. It hadn't snowed much since that first large snowfall in the second week of December, only about six or eight inches. Today there would be about six inches the meteorologist had said, and coupled with the wind, the lake would be a crusted sea of snow waves. You could tell that this year would bring a renewal to all life on earth. Maybe this would be the year of the white buffalo calf.

Elizabeth rose the next morning. Looking out from the loft she took out her pen and pencil, and notebook.

Waves

Hard and crusty,

blinding white,

       the orb reflects what came last night.

Unmarked water,

flowing south,

       hides the traces of any life.

But wait,

on horizon deep with blue,

       a form of magnificent wing.

Come, oh totem

from the north,

       bring the ring of life.

-Elizabeth Washburn


Darkness

Blew whitening night.

Bringing sense of how to live.

Sense of balanced life.

-Elizabeth Washburn

After an hour of writing poetry, having her morning cup of coffee, and a hearty bowl of oatmeal, she decided to go play in the freshly fallen snow with cold crisp air all around. Her long time companion, Aussie Dog, had loved to play in the snow. First she would shovel the front deck, then its steps, all the while throwing the snow at Aussie who leapt to catch it. Today she would still shovel, without her companion, then end the day plowing the upper drive and down to the shore. The snow would be too heavy for the blower. She knew Hal would be down soon, plowing her out and ready for worshiping the almighty coffee cup. She dressed in her winter down-filled jacket and hat, with ear muffs underneath, and mittens; as it was only 10 degrees today.

Heaving and puffing a little from age, she lifted each shovelful over the railing. The snow crunched and squeaked beneath her feet. Her cheeks turned rosy from the work and the frosty air. Nose dripping, Elizabeth had to frequently take breaks to use the tissue stuffed into her jacket pockets. She was sweating now and decided to peel down to her heavy woolen sweater and long polypropylene underwear. A great invention of modern technology, the underwear wicked the sweat away from her body. Just then the sound of the plow came echoing through the woods.

"How you doing Hal?" Elizabeth shouted over the sound of the motor.

"Happy as can be, Elizabeth," he answered, shutting down the plow. "Plowin's been easy today. Not many people out and about yet. Guess there was too much partying last night. When I was down at the village store this morning, I heard the Green boys runs off the road and almost killed themselves. Had to be airlifted to the cities."

"That's just terrible, but I can't help notice you are just talking up a storm this morning. Must be something in this nice fresh air. I have been writing most of the morning. Just couldn't stop either."

"Say do yous want to come over and have a sit down in front of the TV today? Gwen would love to see yous."

"No thanks. I've got a lot of work to do here. Would you like a cup of coffee now? I believe the fresh pot is ready. I made it strong just like you like it. "

"Sounds good to me."

Elizabeth put out some homemade biscuits, too, with real fresh butter.

"How's your goose doing? Must have been hard on her last night."

"I don't know! What's wrong with me! I didn't even check on her yet today. I'm sure she's in the nest though, but I had better get her some corn. I guess I just didn't want to spoil the view by tracking up the lake."

"Did you hears that goose the other night? I couldn't believe it but Gwen and I actually broke into song at one point. Can yous believe it?"

"Yes, because I did too. It was eerie but beautiful."

"Well, I gots to get going. More drives to plow. Thanks for the biscuits and coffee and Happy New Year, Elizabeth."

"Happy New Year to you and Gwen too, and thanks for the invitation. Maybe next time. I'll walk out with you as I haven't even finished my shoveling."

"I noticed. Sure you didn't celebrate a little last night, too?"

They laughed together at the thought.

Elizabeth once again dressed, putting her jacket back on since she had cooled off. After finishing the deck and steps, she walked around the house to the stoop and steps out back and then shoveled a path to the drive. She was exhausted and came in for lunch. Napping soon after her meal, she didn't wake until 2 p.m. to begin plowing.

The plowing was a little harder than she thought it would be. The snow had melted from the sun and had become very heavy. It stuck to the blade and she had to bang the blade down several times to clear it. The day was waning as she finished at the lake turnaround.

There was no goose and Elizabeth had forgotten to check.

· · ·

Elizabeth woke with the first light of the day. In fact, she even caught the sunrise. She had not slept well, as a vision of her goose in trouble came creeping into her dreams. She ate a quick breakfast and flew out the door to the pole barn. Getting on her sled and with a pail full of corn, she made a path of yellow beads as she headed toward the platform. The goose was not there. Elizabeth went around the platform, making a large circle so she didn't get too close to the edge of the water. No goose in the water either. Now she was really worried.

Automatically she gathered all the traits of Wisdom Walking, the crones, and all the traits from the drawing place of the true wisdom of the north. She could see the Great Mountain and the Sacred Lake, where dwelt all her intellectual gifts. Everything told her the goose would go somewhere there was food, she was sure. That meant three places: the small strip island, the large island, or the peninsula. She opted for the peninsula as that was where she had cleared the largest area for food. She went back to the house, put on her gaiters, grabbed her snow shoes, strapped them onto the back of the sled and took off.

She tramped the snow and even dug old trapping areas on the peninsula for over an hour, but all she found were beaver traps left over from years gone by. Since the small island was between the peninsula and the large one, she stopped there next. Even though she covered it inch by inch, it didn't take her as long as the peninsula. Her last resort was the large island before checking along the shoreline. She hoped she was right.

Elizabeth started on the north side. Walking carefully, traveling in small increments from side to side, she looked like someone with a hangover. It was hard on her eyes, even with her sunglasses on, as the snow reflected the sunlight. After an hour she had covered only a third of the island. Then she remembered something she had been taught a long time ago by a camera hunter. A goose nest always faced south. Her stomach was grumbling but she was determined to find the goose if she could.

Elizabeth began at the south end this time, and again moving side to side she scanned the ground for any traces of a goose; poop, feathers, anything. Nothing. When she was beginning to give up hope of finding her, she detected a movement out of the corner of her eye. It was about a foot away. Whatever it was, it didn't try to run. Hoping against hope, she went over to the site. There was the goose; trapped, disheveled, and wide-eyed. As she stepped closer she was aware of the trust it exhibited. Maybe it was envisioning the Great Mountain, too.

Elizabeth laid her hands on the with no problem. Then she took off her gloves and began melting the snow around her. She did not have enough warmth in her hands and went back to the house as fast as she could, boiled water, covered the kettle and rushed back to melt the snow. It seemed like it took an hour. The goose looked frantic when she returned. Elizabeth gradually melted the packed snow and picked her up gently. She set her down gently and stood back, thinking she would fly away back to the sanctuary of the platform and the nest. The goose collapsed. Elizabeth had to get her to water and give her some food. She knew the goose could at least float.

Gathering her in her arms she went as fast as she dared drive with one hand. Stopping her sled dangerously close to the edge of the ice, she got on her belly, and pushed the goose toward the water. It worked. Soon she was sticking her head in for gulps of water. When it looked as if she had had her fill, the goose flew up onto the edge of the ice and was able to get out, though a bit clumsily, and eat.

Elizabeth went back to the house to eat. It was nearly 1:30. Exhausted herself, she had a bowl of soup and crackers and then napped for about twenty minutes. All afternoon Elizabeth tended to the goose. She made trails on the lake, relentlessly uncovered stubble, and laid out corn. Not wanting to wait until tomorrow, Elizabeth decided she would venture out to the farm about ten miles from her to get six bales of hay. She had an idea.

# Chapter 9

The goose had been dying. She had been parched and her bodily functions had shut down. Preparing to join her ancestors she had been practicing detachment before Elizabeth came. The balance of life had been upset and she was totally living the ways of the Medicine Wheel North. She sought freedom from fear, freedom from love, freedom from knowledge; all gifts of the northern traveler. She sought to forget the love of her family, the love from the crone, the knowledge of how to fly, to eat, and to survive. These were the gifts that had been given when one had completed a cycle; these were the gifts practiced when near the end of one's life. Although most geese have a lifespan comparable to a cat, she realized her misjudgment in staying north this winter; her life would be cut short at three. As she was having the vision of the end, she saw the crone on the caterpillar coming across the white; or maybe it was an illusion. She wanted to express that she was here so she tried to ho-onk, but she was too weak. All she could do was sit and hope the crone would find her. She would stay strong in mind and spirit. It was hard when she saw the crone going to the other land. Then she came to the island. But once again the wisdom of the crone was failing; she was on the other end. She tried to ho-onk one more time but it was too much. The energy she had left had failed. Hoping against hope, as she started to drift to the other side, she felt the presence she had known would come. But just as soon as the crone laid hands on her, she left.

In goose time, the warmth seemed another night long wait away. Finally came the lift, and the cradling in the crone's wings, as she felt herself go limp. When the gift of rescue came, it felt like White Buffalo Woman coming to save her as she did her people so long ago; the people of the north for whom the goose became their totem. How great was the gift of life? This crone must be very wise after all. Soon she was drinking water, slowly as her instincts told her, and when she felt the strength she gave a last ditch flutter and made it to the corn. She would take time to reflect on the second life she had now been given, but first she ate her fill. Her bodily functions returned about two hours later, and then she slept the sleep of peace.

. . .

Every day it seemed to be a little warmer to the goose, although the temperature remained in the 20's. Perhaps it was her thankfulness for life and the memory she had of the blowing white. She was back to her usual routine. She would eat, poop, and eat some more. Then she would drink and loaf in her nest for a while.

One day the crone was at the island again, the island that called her every night. At night she was always apprehensive if the wind blew or the snow fell because the pull felt even stronger then. That day, though, the crone had something she was pulling behind her with many interesting items in it. The goose flew over to the woods on the island, confident that she would not be seen as she hid among the brush.

The crone took six large blocks of hay from the trailer. Working slowly, she made a "U" shape in the white, stacked two high on three sides. She put a flat piece of wood on top. The opening faced south. This pleased the goose very much when the crone put more hay in the shelter, as she knew it was another nest for her. She wondered, though, why there was no shiny thing with the grasses she knew so well. As soon as the crone was gone the goose investigated the structure. This actually seemed much better than her other nest, even though it was a long way from the water.

She spent that night in this new magical place and the island no longer called to her.

# Chapter 10

One clear day, after taking care of the goose, Elizabeth went snowmobiling with her friends for the weekend. She shouldn't have to check on the goose for two days as the weather was predicted to be clear. Today was Friday and it would be especially quiet in the woods. She was happy her friends had been able to come up early and make the weekend into three days. This was the most delightful weather to snowmobile in. The temperatures were cold enough so the snow wouldn't melt, yet the sun was warm enough to make the journey most pleasant. She could probably even flip her helmet shield up, although she would still need her hand warmers on.

As Elizabeth made her preparations that morning, gathering helmets and bibs and mittens for everyone, she remembered the last time Sarah had come up and they had gone out with Hal and Gwen.

Hal had known all the trails since he was a groomer. He knew the connecting lakes like the back of his hand. Hal led the four of them into the pine woods of the northern most trails of Wyngate county. She had followed Hal, with Sarah behind her and Gwen bringing up the rear. Thus they rode with Hal and Elizabeth making stops when the other two were no longer in their rear view mirrors. The snow was new and freshly groomed, just as today's would be. They went over crystallized brooks, through swamps filled with dead cattails, up and over hills of powder, through farmers' fields, and disappeared into the close trails lined with the sentinel stately pines with coats of white. They stopped for bathroom breaks and for coffee or water. The only time they had some alcohol was when they stopped for lunch. The hunter's stew just demanded an ice cold beer. As the last of the sun streaked through the trees, they came out onto the last quarter mile to home. The feeling Elizabeth left with had never been matched.

. . .

Once everyone was suited up, including her friend Jan, and they went out to start their machines. Elizabeth started hers and Jan, who drove the 2-up, started hers. One by one they roared in a harmonic tune. Soon they were out on the trails; this day would be their own adventure. Elizabeth had been given a well marked trail map by Hal, which she referred to when they would come to stop signs along the way. They wound through the woods, under the fresh smelling pine, up and down hills, and across marshes. When necessary, the trails would cross lakes. They were well marked, as were the trails in the woods, with orange flags, so a sledder would be safe and stay away from the dangerously thin ice, usually where the streams fed into the lake.

Oh, did Elizabeth love it when they had to go across the smooth thick black ice. Even though the speed limit was 55, just like on the roads, she would buzz along easily at 60 or better. What a thrill that was still, even at her age, banging against the ice. Of course nowdays, she used her back brace.

When hunger struck they would make sure there was a bar and grill nearby for some Snow Shoe Grog or beer to warm themselves and chili or pizza for a hearty meal. They knew where all of these establishments were no matter what trail they were on and planned accordingly.

Today they stopped at Snow and Go, a favorite, and the first thing they did was head for the bathroom.

It was a comical sight in the ladies room. First the women had to remove their jackets so they could get to their bibs. These they left on the pegs outside along with their helmets and mittens. Then they had to lower their bulky bibs. They looked like snow people melting in the spring as the disrobing revealed their true figures.

They sat with a group of people, at the other end of a long picnic-like table, for their meal and drinks. Elizabeth decided not to have her usual drink and went with a hot toddy instead. Sarah had her usual cold one, as she called it, and Jan had coffee. All of them ate chili.

"Sarah, I'm so glad you could take time off from work today and come up for the weekend. How's work going, anyway?" Elizabeth asked her good friend.

"Well, we've started another new program that will save all of our kids from going uneducated. It's called 'Save a Mind.' It is primarily the same as any other we've ever done. The major difference is that instead of covering just Language Arts and Mathematics, it also recognizes the need for Science and History. The Freshmen work on a team, with teachers who meet on their prep to plan the lessons for the week; they also check everyday for glitches. The kids do take their mathematics off team, though, due to the different levels at which they work. I will be happy, though, when this project is over and I can get back to my winter home in Arizona. I still love being connected to the schools but the flying is a bit too much. I may limit my consulting to Arizona only next year."

"Sounds very interesting. I gather you work on a team?"

"Actually, no. I work with the upper class students."

"How did you get that assignment?" asked Jan, who lived on a farm down the road.

"Simple. I have seniority. I had been at Central for 27 years before retiring."

"Yes, and do you remember the fun we had way back in the 70's?" Elizabeth asked.

"Oh, yes!", and the two of them began to laugh.

Not wanting to leave Jan out of the conversation, they related their pranks over the last of their meal.

After paying their bill, they once again hit the trails. They passed through fields with gates, pine tree lined forest trails, and over lakes and streams until they saw Elizabeth's home. It had been a majestic day. Even though they were really tired, each told a story about their favorite part. Jan enjoyed riding the hills of the other farmer's fields. She knew many of these people from get-togethers but had never been to their fields. Now, she said, she would have another topic of conversation. Since Jan was so quiet to begin with, Elizabeth thought any topic would be a blessing to her. Sarah loved the Norwegian pines. She said they reminded her of her home. She sounded almost homesick when she related stories of how her father had cleared away many of these trees to build her childhood home. Of course Elizabeth's favorite part was playing at being a snowmobile racer. That, she said, had been her secret dream ever since she had seen her first machine. Sarah and Jan laughed and told her it really wasn't a secret. Everyone could see it in her eyes. As the stories came to an end, Jan left and Sarah and Elizabeth got comfortable for the night. Finally, with teacups in hand, they sat quietly, enjoying each others' company and listening to the news and weather on the radio. It sounded like another storm was headed their way.

# Chapter 11

The sense of winter seemed to last forever. The constant smell of pine in the woods and the touch of cold on one's lungs as she breathed in the icy air, affirmed this claim. When Elizabeth and the goose breathed it in they could taste the crystals on their tongue. There was the sound of the rumbling ice as it shifted from the weight of the snow and the chill of the nights penetrating cold. On clear nights, when the conditions were favorable, no icy fingers trailing into their lungs or groans from the heaving ice would keep the two ladies from their play. In the moonlit, crow-black nights each could be seen dancing the dance of a dream. At these times they became one with the North.

The skies turned gray and dark often that winter. Anyone needing sunlight had to consciously get out of the house and exercise to offset the depression often associated with life in the Northern climates. Elizabeth had come to live with the clouds and was never far away from a diversion. Now, the sun moved past its lowest point and the days promised a blue freeze. The temperature sat somewhere between -30 and -20 degrees for about 3 days. Even though this had the effect of putting a temporary end to outside activities, Elizabeth found consolation in the fact that spring would be just two months away. She could see it in the life all around her and wrote often about this transition of seasons; a transition she rarely shared with any of her friends as they were determined to believe winter would hang on forever.

Transitions

Why do you hibernate

so long; beneath

your coats of steel?


Why not see the other side

of sun white upon the face?

The long days gone,

with the passing

of two months gaiety.


Take up your voice

find your song,

sing the dance,

of new days coming

bright and warm.

-Elizabeth Washburn


This unusual cold sent the goose into a hibernating state where it lay with its head and legs folded under; it didn't eat. Thanks to Elizabeth's resolve, however, when the temperature once again climbed out of the minuses there was always plenty to eat on the snowmobile packed trails.

The snowfall had set a record for the winter months and with March, the snowiest month, still more than one long month away, it was predicted to top out at 65 inches. That would be at least 15 inches above the annual average, but given the icy glare that winter had bestowed the past four years, the snow had been welcomed. All the winter businesses were flourishing and it also meant the lake levels would be up and the summer businesses would enjoy the benefits as well.

By mid-February Elizabeth had readied herself for another spring greeting. Since the days were now cold, then warm from the ever nearing sun, it was time to perform the ceremony of the crone which was directed toward releasing the fertile promises of the Earth and the warmth hidden therein. The focus was the strength of her darkened seeds being bared, soon to be summoned by the Sun of spring. The ceremony was conducted in the same room, in a similar way to that of January's, but with different items on the table. The chant brought dreams of the sun, sharing of warmth of breath, and sweetness of a brightened sleep.

February was not the same in the northern climates, as in the southern, and Elizabeth knew, as did all crones, that here the seeds would not be bared soon. However, there were dates on which these ceremonies had to be performed, and she never failed to abide by them.

· · ·

March had come in just as promised; snow, rain, mix, and more snow. The temperatures would climb to the mid 30's then plummet to the low 20's. The freezing and melting were taking their toll on all natures' creatures and creations.

Then before she knew it, the crone ceremonies for the Vernal Equinox were at hand. They were held at the New Moon in March. Once again many items were gathered for the table just after the crescent Moon of March was setting in the evening.

On the day of the night of the event, the strength of Earth is roused as the Sun returns. This is a glad event and there is great rejoicing about attending their nuptials. The Earth comes forward with its sleeping bounty to join the Sun at the altar of air.

In the late evening the table was covered in a cloth of bright yellow with twelve yellow candles in a single row. There was a sheaf of whites of a willow tree bound with a yellow ribbon, a brass bell, sandalwood incense, oil, plain sandalwood, sweet golden wine, and a goblet all precisely arranged before the candles.

Elizabeth chanted many words, including a moving one bringing an end to sleep and night; wakening of the life in the earth, and the sun. It ended with the words:

WE ARE THE SUN,

WE ARE THE EARTH,

CIRCLES OF FIRE,

CIRCLES OF SKIN.


SPRING IS OUR MARRIAGE,

SPRING IS WHERE WE LIE,

SO IN THIS SPRING

OUR SOULS ARE WED.

**JOINED FOREVER AND FOREVER**

**EVEN THOUGH DARK AUTUMN AND WINTER**

**WILL COME.**

. . .

March, traditionally, is said to be the snowiest month of the year. At this time of the year it is said that there is always a storm on the weekend of the high school boy's basketball tournament. Just as predictable as the sunrise, though a bit late, 10 more inches of snow fell the Monday after the tournament. That brought the total for that month to 14.3 inches. Elizabeth could still snowmobile but the snow would continue to melt almost daily now. The worst of winter was probably over.

Elizabeth walked and skied on the lake and in the woods almost every day now. The shush of the skis gliding over the surface of the corn snow along snowshoe packed paths, the smell of the warm 35 degree air, and the taste of the few tapped maple syrup trees, drifting in to touch her tongue as she breathed, made her smile. The ice would be too thin now to snowmobile and was beginning to groan under her weight. The sun was warmer, and as it streamed through the tree tops it sparked the earth with a feeling that lit the soul.

# Chapter 12

The goose sang in her musical voice, "When will all this white stop coming down?" She wanted to be closer to her water but the shiny nest was still filled with snow. She still saw the crone out walking when her feet grew or sliding when they became long ones; she always dropped corn for her. She was thankful.

Then one day something happened; the white began to change. The sun was out; a shining yellow orb which thoroughly warmed her body. She saw the white stuff was disappearing a little and it felt sticky beneath her feet. When it did snow again it felt like little pebbles of sand. Four beautiful warm days made her hopeful the white would be gone; then the temperatures dropped below freezing again. But the goose could tell by the soft crone-hand smell of the air, that it wouldn't last long.

She ventured back to the platform at that time. It felt really comfortable to be in her familiar nest again and to be this close to the water and the corn. She ate and drank and ate and drank some more, sometimes by diving for it, sometimes going to the island, and sometimes she just ate the corn. Then she pooped nearly two pounds as she did everyday she was alive. Fortunately for the crone it sank into the melting snow.

One day, as the white stuff was rapidly disappearing, the crone started distributing the corn on shore without any reason. The goose found this strange, but it didn't matter as long as she could eat. The big turtle with the big mouth came around a lot less now, only when it became whiter again. She didn't know turtles only liked to eat white stuff in the winter. So that is how they stayed alive. Everything about the crone and life here was curious to the goose but she had become accustomed to living with it.

One day toward the end of March, it rained. Now the goose had seen rain before but was amazed at the amount of the white stuff that left that day. The lake, however, stayed frozen and added another very slippery surface that night. When the goose tried to leave her nest the next day, she looked like a puppy trying to run on a wooden floor and she went sliding into the water.

. . .

The afternoon was quite warm for March, even though snow remained on the ground. Elizabeth went out on the deck with her notebook and the tools of the poet. She wrote in the warmth of the sun, although a lined jacket was needed over her sweatshirt because of the breeze.

Magic

Sending down warm rays.

Purely satisfying day,

Whisk white stuff away.

Breath of smell sending.

Breeze fully penetrating.

Spring is coming now.

Having ice go out.

Satisfying all the birds.

Revealing lake of turquoise blue.

Eagles and geese will abound.

Eating fish and grasses deep.

Deaden life and life anew.

-Elizabeth Washburn

Elizabeth watched that day and anticipated spring. She was tired of winter now, it was always so long. She sat there until dusk, just writing, with only a break for lunch. Even though she occasionally shivered it didn't matter.

March had been a snowy month, as Elizabeth had predicted, and even though the calendar said spring was here, it still felt like winter most days. She was still able to sauna, roll in the snow, and spa every morning. Even though the sun tried to melt the snow during the day, the frosty temperatures kept it around at night. The last of the snow would be eaten up, finally, by the sun and rain as the temperatures began to stay above freezing during the day. Now it was a matter of waiting for the weather to warm enough to melt the ice.

One morning toward the middle of April, the ice would go out and sink into the water beneath it. Unfortunately, the temperature would go down to 22 degrees, or some other below-freezing temperature, at night and there would be a light skim of ice on the lake the next morning. As the temperatures would rise during the morning hours, the water warmed and the ice would be gone again. Before long, it would soon be gone for good, and not return. Yes, Elizabeth knew spring was coming and so were the April rains. She wrote:

Secrets

You, calm holder

of the change

source of all beginnings,

show me your truths,

your underpinnings.

You, molted mirror

of the seasons,

once rippled with mother's

icy breath,

show me calm

and show me strife.

You, must show me

what geese see.


Is it their image

burning frozen

or mirrors' reflecting life?

Flying by

can they see,

far below the surface dive?

You, must yield to me

what geese see.

-Elizabeth Washburn


<u>Write Your Story</u>

Through the window

Twilight dawns.

You yawn.

    Diving into

    Water clear.

    You peer.

Meeting self

Are you aware,

Who is there?

    Can you

Find who you are,

Purity or marred?

-Elizabeth Washburn


<u>On my way</u>

On the water blue,

sailing to the shore with woods,

come about to me.

-Elizabeth Washburn

Book 2

The
Spring

## **The Geese**

They came from

South

on wind smell

fresh;

tails streaming

jets,

brushing above

trees.

Taking roost, as if to stay,

on turquoise

waters;

a reunion-party,

a goose-music

band played

through the

night.

    A goose guided

    North

    at first sun's

    light.

-Elizabeth Washburn

# Chapter 1

Elizabeth knew every word on the paper she held would always be seen as 'just Elizabeth'.

. . .

Unseen forces melted the lake from underneath and the crone waited for the cracked shoreline to recede. Elizabeth stopped venturing out to the ice and the goose did not understand. She cried some nights for the companionship and extra corn the crone had given her. New shoots of vegetation started to appear all over the peninsula and small island alike and the goose, in her quest for new food, understood. She started flying to the farmers' fields. Then she was overjoyed and paraded herself about when Elizabeth provided her corn on the land, when the white stuff remained on shore.

Rain and sun continued to work on the top of the ice, until one day the goose noticed open areas of water around its perimeter. She swam almost all the way around that day taking time to dive and look for vegetation she had not had all winter. She enjoyed her new found freedom. One day, as she was setting down, the ice disappeared from under her. She was able to swim across the lake to eat some corn that had been covered by the early winter snow, and was as seasonably overwhelmed as a couple of high school kids on their way to school on a beautiful sunny morning. She was again floating, alone and happy, and sang out a short bar of goose music. As she sang, Elizabeth was on her deck as if to confirm the beauty of her song: she was performing a peculiar dance. The goose sang her song and the crone danced her dance and they became one with their beloved lake again. What a glorious day, the two kindred spirits would have agreed.

. . .

As if on cue, a gaggle of geese flew in the next week welcoming spring: their unmistakable voices filling the air one evening, in their V-shaped chorus line, and splashing down as the choreographer had taught them to do. They preened and sang, once again enjoying the reunion, waltzing as if they were at their spring prom. The goose had only to dance too. She did as they did: she flapped her wings, moved her feet, and swam in circles. The goose was bursting with pride at not being afraid anymore. Soon the lake filled until the small prom turned into a ball, just as there had been last fall. Some of the families stayed through the night while others just stopped by for the dance. Night after night for nearly a month they danced and they visited, then gracefully left as they took to the sky and continued their long journey north. Two pairs stayed to begin their new families; the goose did not know she would be a third, and just delighted in the season as she sensed she was part of some new and wonderful plan.

Thoreau had called Canada geese, "grenadiers of the air...coming to unlock the fetters of northern rivers," and their nasal quavering chant heralded the arrival of Spring as the warm days were ushered in. Daily they could be seen feasting in the fields and on the shore, but at night they returned to the lake. Some were two and three year olds that had flown north and were separated, just as the goose had been, from their families.

Ganders, unattached, were looking to find a mate and the goose flaunted herself like a princess whenever they were in her view. When they came near her, as several often did, they made a huge fuss amongst themselves. The ganders' dance was a carbon copy of a dance from *West Side Story*. As they got closer they would spread their wings, flip their tails, and stand tall in the water. They hissed and challenged each other like members of warring gangs. There was much posturing and flapping of wings; spreading them as far out from their body as possible, as wide as a man could reach from finger tip to finger tip. Then one gander would try to get closer to the goose. The others, however, would form a barrier, not letting him get any better position than any of the others had. The goose realized that one of these showoffs would probably become *her gander mate* and had goose bumps at the thought of it.

. . .

The days became filled with community time. At the reunion, the older geese would pass down the stories of the ancestors. The younger geese would gather around the elders during the loafing to hear stories of the old ones that had come before. The old ones had not passed down all their stories for they were too painful for the next generations to bear. Had she had access to these stories the goose might have known why she became the totem for Elizabeth. However, as the goose listened intently, as she had before, she finally understood that many, many years before humans arrived in North America, the geese had always signaled the change of the seasons for all the other birds and animals of the North. In the fall, all things of nature would observe their arrival from the north and begin to prepare for the cold months ahead. The squirrels would begin to gather their nuts and the bear would start to look for their perfect bed for the winter. The deer would teach the ways of the hunter to their fawns as the fawns lost their spots. The buck would begin to grow bumps that would eventually become a full rack of antlers. Even the caterpillars would become involved in telling the seasonal change by growing wide or narrow black stripes. And as the oaks began to drop their acorns, the deciduous trees would show their true colors as one last stand before the pines became the foreground of winter's wonderland.

In the spring they would bring the news to all the birds on their way north. The snowbirds would follow, their beloved songs heard as the earth warmed. When they arrived the bear would come out of hibernation and begin looking for food to feed their now thin bodies. The squirrels would also look to find a supplement to their nut diet. The caterpillars would form cocoons as the days warmed and the deer would begin to have their first fawns. And the fish would begin to spawn.

Geese knew this story, but the predictions that their flight pattern was a sign of early or late spring, early or late winter, made the modern day geese laugh, for they did not know its truth and were sure the elders embellished. Elizabeth, like others who were akin to the geese, knew the sign of the geese was true because her mother had passed it to her; she could not explain it. The native peoples had coexisted successfully for millennia and they knew; so Elizabeth knew, in an unconscious way. This may have contributed to the spirit of the goose totem.

. . .

One of the more disturbing stories the geese heard in those days of migration had to do with some humans. The goose talked to the Great Spirit about the crone and realized she was not one of these humans after hearing the story.

In the last thirty years their migration had been disrupted by humans; in some places it would never be the same again. The humans had left lakes open in the winter, as did the crone, so the knowledge of the migratory paths had been lost to thousands of geese. The elder geese told of the flyways and how it was important to keep your family with the gaggle. If you were lured by the thought of easy winters and not having to forage for food you should think again, for to stay might mean your eventual death.

The goose knew this was an important story for her because she had not gone south last winter. She knew that if she had lost all that her mother and father had taught her she might spend all her winters here and she wasn't sure that was what she should do. She wondered why staying might mean her eventual death, for the crone had seemed to be kind. She listened on.

In the year of the turn of the century many species of wildlife, not just geese, had disappeared and many more were on the brink of extinction. Killing seemed feasible and the population of geese was believed to be inexhaustible. Then there came a time when the killing lessened, but not long enough. In the middle years the giant Canada goose was thought to be extinct and the other species of geese cried. The great spirit, though, had shown the way for one pair to outwit the slaughter and some humans began to protect them. As they became more plentiful, there was an effort to restore them to other areas by rounding them up during their annual molt, a time when they cannot fly. They were shipped to various protected lakes, far away from where they knew how to fly, and had to establish new breeding populations. This was a period of great mourning, but they adapted to their new habitats. Within thirty years there was an abundance of geese and new flyways were formed. As the geese flew and landed on unprotected lakes another terrible atrocity began.

The goose knew the rest of the story; there were terrible roundups for slaughter and relocations to hunting areas. Many of her ancestors had lost family to these inhumane acts. She was pleased she did not live then but sad to have lost parts of her history.

. . .

Elizabeth's goose did not know the rest of the story; this was a DNR lake, a management habitat which established a solution to these practices. The shoreline gave the preferred walk between water and land and other grazing areas during molting and escorting goslings. The grass and shrubs, even though growing as little as 18 inches high in a 10 foot band, acted as a deterrent to geese in areas they were not desired, like other peoples land, and impeded their access to grazing as well as blocking their view from predators. The only down side, that the goose had not yet experienced, was there was still limited hunting in the fall.

. . .

<u>Magnificence</u>

honkers

flying

formation

known

routes

precise

time

spring

herald

north

-Elizabeth Washburn

# Chapter 2

While the geese told their stories, Elizabeth had her chores neatly listed on paper, and as the March and April days became warmed by the smile of the spring sun, she knew there were many to complete before she could plant: the highlight of spring. So she had begun counting the days until Mothers' Day, the earliest date she would chance planting without a frost. As she looked over her list she was sure, as she was every year, that it had grown.

1. dock
2. aerator
3. tractor
4. plow, blower equipment
5. snowmobiles
6. remove leaves left from fall
7. window wells
8. water pump
9. buy plants, May
10. buy stain for deck when on sale
11. Marvin wash windows, incl. traps.
12. Gary, spray insects April
13. motorcycle, boat motors
14. bird feed, corn for goose(?)
15. pull up plant leaves that didn't survive
16. deer barrier, hostas
17. remove wood near house: pile 50 feet away

Looking at the list made her tired but she would try to do a little something today.

Elizabeth took the canisters of food for the birds and placed them on the hand sleigh she used to distribute the seed to the feeders. She had seen a robin, just the other day, and knew the other birds would be close behind. She was going to put up the feeders again this year even though there had been trouble from the bear last spring. She could not blame the bear, they were hungry from a winter of hibernation. She would just take them down each night until food for the bear became plentiful. The goose would do fine when the new vegetation began to sprout; since the snow was melted enough she could get to the farmers' fields to eat again, so Elizabeth distributed just a minimal amount of corn on shore.

It had been a relatively warm day, and Elizabeth had chosen not to wear her long underwear. She had chosen correctly, because she became very warm while she was restacking the wood pile from down below into the new area. She didn't need a secondary source of heat now, even though the temperatures at night still dipped below freezing; she would just use her forced air furnace. The logs were removed first. Then she moved the supports. With each bend of her legs Elizabeth had let out another grunt. As she finished the task her back said it was time to soak in the spa. She removed her back brace and had a short but relaxing soak, pleased that she was still fit enough to see this tedious undertaking through. When she emerged from the spa it was about 5 p.m. time to have her customary glass of wine; spring was wine season to Elizabeth. Music from Lorie Line came softly from the CD as she put her feet up. Just about dark she heard the goose music. She turned off the CD player and listened; the cheese and crackers were left uneaten next to her chair.

The new moon let the starlight twinkle even more brightly that evening. Elizabeth climbed the stairs to the loft and gazed out through the trapezoid windows and said to the darkening room, "What a gorgeous night." Finally, her eyes couldn't focus any more and she found her way downstairs without a flashlight in hand. Sitting in the recliner she relaxed, curling up in a lap blanket, and took out <u>The Nature Reader</u>, edited by Daniel Halpern and Dan Frank. It appealed to her renewed seasonal senses. The first story, <u>The Nature Writer's Dilemma</u>, by John Hay, explained that the word nature comes from the Latin, *to be born*. This was something Elizabeth understood as she was annually born again this time of the year. The medicine wheel was in the East, and the journey had started once again. She pondered these teachings at great length before her eyes became heavy with sleep.

When Elizabeth saw the first light that night she recalled the teachings of the East. East is the direction of illumination. Light comes into the world. Therefore, East is the direction of guidance and leadership. It is here that one acquires beautiful clear speech and the ability to help others to understand. The discernment to see clearly through complex situations is learned. Much of what a crone knows and passes on to other generations starts in the East. Elizabeth had learned the first steps of how to be a good leader here before, and to see things as they are connected to all other things: to be self-reliant, to have hope for all people, and to trust her vision, but with each new year their meaning deepened. Traveling South, West, and North are important in learning the rest about leadership and complete another journey. Like the seasons, the time had come to travel the circle again.

• • •

The crone ceremony on the New Moon of April was one of Elizabeth's favorites. Her eyes were bright and clear as she put her book down the next morning and remembered the chants. They involved recognizing the mother of mothers, of waters, and green leaves. Mother holds the waters of sky, of birth, of sea, and earth. She also bears the leaves, the season, the green child. The child is ourselves. Her name is given by the earth, by water, by us. It is our name, the name is **Life**. Life as she knew it was tied to this season of rebirth and new-found leadership. All of her people's teachings, all of the lessons of the earth's animals, and all of the wisdom of the crone were evident in her face.

• • •

**A Charm for Eternal Youth**

"Go to a grove of pines, when the Moon is new, and in the Earth beneath their boughs inscribe a circle, wide as you are tall. Lie down within it, your arms extended to meet the circles rim, and say these words:

THE ANCIENT PINE

IS EVERGREEN

THE CRESCENT MOON

MAY NEVER WANE

THE CIRCLE BOUND

IS EVER ROUND

AND SO MY LIFE

AS LIGHT AND LEAF

Pluck three needles of pine from a green branch, take them home, and wind them tightly round about with a hair from your head and a long green thread. Keep this charm beside your bed, that you may dream of eternity, and each night before you sleep, repeat the words that have conjured youth from the enchanted grove. Ever after, you should wear some token of green-jade, emerald, or other stone, ornament, or article of clothing-in honor of these fair spells now threaded through your life." From **THE CRONE'S BOOK OF WISDOM** by Valerie Worth; one of Elizabeth's favorite books since becoming a crone; she had it memorized.

• • •

Elizabeth had been blessed to be a crone and an Indian. She had a new level of understanding after performing the crone ceremony and recalling the teachings of the Medicine Wheel. She was filled with joy and hope as she led the birds to their food. Light had come into the world. She wrote about this wonderful season of life the following morning.

Complexity of the Web

To be born,

light illuminates,

new day coming.

Belief in the mother

her knowledge passed.

When the child loves

there is no name but life.

Speech, like the songs

of the nightingale,

helping the child

to understand.

As courage is born,

truthfulness begins:

warmth of spirit,

purity,

hope.

The unquestioning

acceptance

adds a new level of

understanding.

-Elizabeth Washburn

Direction

East beginnings.

A mother of mother's child.

Mother of waters. Holds waters of sky.

Bears the season of green children.

Waters of sky and birth.

-Elizabeth Washburn

That night Elizabeth dreamed the dream of the East in a vision.

. . .

Spring was coming as foretold by the geese; Elizabeth could see spring in the air the next morning as it flew in on sine wave currents. There was a dampness as the frost left the trees and Elizabeth dressed in her usual wool shirt, jeans, boots, and floppy hat. Her gloves hung out of her pocket. It was a warm 48 degrees by the time she emerged from the house, having taken care of inside chores earlier that morning. She decided to service the snowmobiles. She had gotten a lot of use out of the second one this year, since many of her friends and Hal's had needed one when they came up North. The plugs had to be greased, oil drained and refilled, filter changed, and new gas, with stabilizer, put in. It took about three hours to complete these two tasks. Elizabeth had gotten up very early, though, so she was finished by noon.

After lunching on a tuna sandwich, a glass of milk, and a banana, she turned her attention to the plow and blower equipment. Elizabeth cleared an area behind the snowmobiles. Seems like she always accumulated boxes over the winter and never put them away until spring. Since she had built shelves in the back of the pole barn she got a ladder and put them up there. She spent the rest of the next two hours plus, maneuvering the blower into its storage spot. She should have left it on one of her tractors, it would have been much easier to move, but she had to do everything the hard way. It was heavy and had only two small wheels to roll it on. Walking to the tractor she took off the plow; she wouldn't be needing that anymore. Fortunately she could get closer to the storage area so she didn't have as far to move it. A few huffs and puffs and it was in place. With equipment now in winter storage, Elizabeth next turned to the tractors. She oiled them and cleaned the plugs. She checked the lines and hoses for any cracks that might have occurred over the winter. Then she put in the new filter. She did this on both tractors so by the time she finished she was so tired she couldn't handle any more chores. Fortunately, the sun still cast enough light that Elizabeth could find her way back to the house. Then, placing her first step up, she caught her foot and fell.

• • •

The goose waited for the eyes to appear and the crone to dance along with her song that night. During her preening and playing with the ganders' attention-seeking tactics, she had only been periodically aware of the crone. She remembered seeing her decorating the trees with miniature nests and seed, not unlike the ones she had built for her. She had seen her pour the seed and in passing gave thought to the dwindling supply of corn. She knew, however, that the seed was for the songbirds brought North by the migrating geese and she really didn't need the corn any more. The last time she was sure the crone was around was when she had heard the turtle's rough voice. Not seeing her now, the goose sang louder and louder until it brought Hal and Gwen out of their place. Looking up the hill toward the nest she saw it stood cold and dark. The goose had grown so used to having her around that she became aware that something was wrong. The eyes always burned bright. She watched and directed the choir this time with a little more quavering in her voice than normal.

• • •

Elizabeth was almost immediately in intolerable pain and she imagined what the goose had gone through those bitter cold winter nights of the big storm, stuck on the island. She felt her leg but already knew it was broken. Whether she could make it inside or not would be a pure act of will. She knew there would be little chance of rescue tonight. No one could see her lights from their homes; no one, not even Hal and Gwen! She would have to make it through the porch and the living room to get to the phone. The five steps must have looked like a mountain to Elizabeth; she would have to rely on her upper body to see her through. The steps had now become slippery slots in the nights frost filled air, adding to the treacherous state of the mission she was about to undertake.

As Elizabeth began, she had a look of desperate determination, knowing that the temperatures would be in the mid 20's tonight; she was not dressed for that kind of night outdoors. She took on a step about every 20 minutes as she strained not to fall backward, the pain in her leg and the burning in her arms preventing a faster pace. As she made her way up she heard loud goose music. Was the goose trying to tell someone she wasn't there in the house? " No, don't be foolish, Elizabeth," she said out loud.

Working up a sweat she finally got to the landing about two hours later. Exhaustion and cold had begun to set in. The hardest part of all was next; how would she unlatch the door? Anyone else would have given up, but not Elizabeth. She looked determined to stand. She had a good leg. Reaching for the crossbars on the railing she pulled herself about five inches up. "God, does it hurt," Elizabeth cried out into the dark woods. Then she rose another five and another five and so on until she reached the top of the railing. She was kneeling on her good leg now with her fingertips barely holding on. With all her might she pulled herself up, putting all her weight on her right leg. She had about a foot and a half to get to the door. Not wanting to fall again, she kept one hand on the rail, the one on the side with the bad leg, which was so painful now she was crying. She made a lunge forward and reached for the door. It was too far away and she began to slip. Fortunately, Elizabeth was able to grab on with both hands and gasped for air. She would have to move closer. Dragging the broken leg, tears streaming down her face, and inching ever nearer, she finally touched it. Supporting herself totally on her good leg, she turned the latch and the door opened. She fell again, shooting excruciating pain through her already broken leg. She lay there and, as the door quietly closed, passed out from the pain.

· · ·

Needing a good cup of coffee while Gwen was at church, Hal decided to go to Elizabeth's to worship the almighty coffee cup and see if she knew what all the commotion was about last night. He walked over along the path, as it was a nice, cool, spring day. You could smell the sweet air and hear the songbirds singing their perfect melodies. Then he thought again of the ruckus the geese had thrown last night and how completely out of tune they would be if they had been singing now. Never a noisier ke-ronking had he heard. It seemed as if they were upset, but he didn't have a clue as to why.

When he arrived at Elizabeth's, things didn't seem right. Usually she would have the tractors out by now and be merrily working away, close to the house, as she awaited their usual routine. He knocked on her door and got no answer. It was unlatched and as he went in, calling for her, he nearly tripped over her limp body. She hardly stirred. It was at that moment that he thought of the goose and how Elizabeth had saved its life; had it been trying to do the same last night? He knew she had said that the goose looked like she watched her sometimes. He looked at Elizabeth again. She was unconscious and her leg was clearly broken. He had to get help. Hal went to the phone and dialed 911. He knew he shouldn't move her. He tried to wake her, but to no avail, as he listened to her shallow breathing. He hurried inside to get her a blanket. It seemed to take forever for the ambulance to arrive. It had to come from Blair and that was nearly 30 miles away. He learned later they had gotten lost when they missed the fire number.

Elizabeth had a little extra weight from the winter, so it was hard to get her on the gurney. After they immobilized her leg, out the door and down the steps they went, slowly as they could. She had awakened by this time and was yelling like Hal had never heard her yell before. When they got her inside the van they started an IV with a pain killer and an oxygen mask, as she was hyperventilating. Later Elizabeth was to tell the story of how she had closed her eyes tight against the pain and visualized canoeing the calm lake waters. It was a natural blood pressure lowering trick and pain reliever taught by her mother. Much to the paramedics surprise she soon calmed down. As they sped away, Hal got his truck, wrote Gwen a note, and went to Blair as fast as he dared on the twisted country roads. He would be there when Elizabeth awoke.

That night there was much ke-ronking on the lake again as the sky began to turn dark. Obviously the goose and all the other geese were trying to alert someone to the fact that the crone was nowhere to be found. Soon however, the lights came on due to a timer that Hal had installed, and the geese settled down. Had Elizabeth known, she would have said for sure, the goose had saved her life.

# Chapter 3

The ganders danced the grandest of dances while the goose swam and preened all day: she looked as if she was about to have a big date. Leading a gander on was great fun to a goose. The ganders held their heads on their elegant necks like men, with their chins stuck forward, each daring the other to hit first. Then they would dance, flipping their tails in defiance, in tune to the hiss of an unusual sound. When the tune had concluded, they would peck as a fighter might jab at his opponent, and flail about with their powerful wings. In response the goose would swim closer and tease, until all the others would fold their necks and get ready for a real attack.

The one that caught her attention, though, didn't look aggressive when his head was protruding. The others didn't take him seriously either, just as he planned. In fact, he looked like he was trying to appease the others while dancing the finest dance. His wings were extended nearly six feet, his feet barely touched the surface, and when he flipped his tail, he flipped it at her in a rather seductive way, rather than defiantly at the other ganders; she felt tingles all over. It was time. The wood ducks observed, as though in judgment, as the goose swam away. They would dive, as if in embarrassment, as she turned her back and worked on looking good for her date.

The magnificent, handsome gander began swimming in a circle around her. The circle got larger in diameter until there were no more challenges from the other ganders. Then the pair began having their own dance. They greeted each other in a triumphant ceremony. Their heads were shaking, necks stretching, and the male and the goose snorted notes in a perfectly timed duet. Then, dipping their heads and necks, they knew copulation would come soon.

. . .

If Elizabeth had been watching she would have written a poem. Instead she was resting comfortably in the hospital with a cast on her leg running from ankle to thigh. "And thank the lord," Della would say to that. The goose, however, was so preoccupied she didn't notice that Elizabeth wasn't around that day.

As night fell, the goose looked up at the crone's nest and happily saw the eyes shinning warmly down the hill. Hal had put two timers in earlier, after he had come back from the hospital. There would be no frantic singing tonight, only the sounds of the mighty ball.

The goose would begin building her nest tomorrow. The goose knew that story all too well. She could have used the crone's platform for the nest if it were more discreetly hidden. It had been just fine for the winter, but the crone had not painted the nest greenish-brown. The water was a little too deep here, off the big island, where her nest could have been; it was almost 6 feet, so that wasn't even an option. A good depth is 2-4 feet. She would find a more sheltered place; one closer to shore, perhaps on the smaller island, on the lakes bank, or in the osprey's nest where the water was more shallow. There she would build the finest nest a goose and a gander had ever had.

For tonight, though, as the sun settled into the horizon she went to the familiar place to spend her night in the water. This time she had company; her gander.

. . .

In the dawn of the morning's, pale, electrified sky the goose reminisced about her own days as a gosling. She was sure she remembered a soft nest as she broke through her shell on that warm, sunny day. Or maybe what she remembered was the warmth of her mother's body bearing down as she struggled for air. Whatever the experience, she was sure about one thing, the nest was cloud-like soft. She wanted to build a nest just like that. She would have to call on the stories of the ancestors.

All day they swam and flew; the gander and the goose tried out different locations to bed down and make a home for their goslings that were sure to appear soon. The osprey's nest proved too high; what if one of the goslings fell? The small island was too close to the water; what if the water rose and swept them all away. The area near the old beaver dam was out because the pair that returned every year, had claimed that spot. They tried the other side of the big island and even thought about the sheltered nest that Elizabeth had built in the season of the ice, but it was not open enough to see predators that may be lurking nearby. Then they found the perfect spot. There was a peninsula that jutted toward the small island and near the waters where the goose had nursed her wounds so long ago. It afforded an open view of the lake to the north, south and the west. It was relatively shallow here, providing for good vegetation and readily accessible building materials. The grasses to the east were higher than they would have liked but they could still walk to land, which was a major requirement. The nest would blend into the natural surroundings and she wouldn't have to worry about intruding on the other families' spaces. She did know she didn't want to be sociable, so this was good for them, too.

So the goose made preparations to build her nest. First she made a ground depression. When completed she went in search of sticks, cattails, reeds, and grasses. Dragging them back to the nest was quite a chore and she wondered where her gander had gotten off to. When she was finished lining the depression she took some time off, floating on the clear azure blue lake. She glanced up to the crone's nest because she had not seen her all day. There was no sound of the turtle she had grown so fond of either, but the eyes were on last night so she knew she was safe.

After a lengthy period of time, to a goose, she went back to her nest where she took her bounty and lined the depression in the ground. It would take more materials than she had brought; it had a 25 inch circumference, so she gathered and went to gather more. Once the lining was completed, the goose made a central cup. The cup had to be big enough for five to seven eggs. It was beautifully, geometrically perfect. The gander said so when he returned from his socializing, and he praised her highly; the scoundrel.

Finally, the goose plucked down from her chest. Even though goose eggs were hardy, she didn't want to take any chance in crushing them when she sat on them throughout the incubation period.

· · ·

The goose laid five creamy colored, matte-finished eggs. The gander guarded them and defended the nest and the surrounding territory from the many predators that might be lurking. The goose lay crouched with her neck extended and still, day after day. Periodically she would stand up and inspect them, turning them gently with her beak, and rearranging the nice soft down cushion. The only time she was away was when she went to eat and swim every morning and evening. It was during this time her eggs were at their greatest danger of being eaten. The goose was young so didn't really understand the danger well and the gander told her. He had learned this from one of the other fathers on the lake. So they became very diligent, in an all knowing way, in looking after their eggs. They were not diligent enough.

· · ·

With little else to do, the goose watched the crone's nest on a daily basis and looked for the night shining eyes. She never heard the turtle. Finally, one day, she saw her sitting on her nest, just as the goose sat on hers. The crone, however, was doing something very odd indeed. She was moving her wings back and forth across something white. The goose wondered if maybe this was the technique she used to incubate her eggs. She hadn't seen the crone leave her nest all day, however, and wondered when she would eat and drink. She had forgotten the crone didn't drink.

Finally, the goose couldn't stand not knowing what was going on and sent the gander over to inspect. He returned to report that the turtle was not around. He also reported there was no sage on the lookout for her well-being and he could have walked right up and stolen her eggs. As he was finishing his report and the goose was settling back down, he started hissing and flailing his wings about. The goose was scared. She kept very, very still, drawing herself into the nest as much as she could. There in the grass, slithering toward the nest, heard but unseen, was a bull snake. The pair had dropped their guard and this particularly fierce predator was about to attack. Just before it reached up to grab at the nest the gander had seen it. He lashed out with his beak. As he did so, the bull snake puffed up his cheeks, trying desperately to get to the eggs. He tried to scare the pair of geese away but their instincts would not allow them to abandon the nest, no matter what harm might come to them. Hissing, biting, slithering, flaying abounded but the gander prevailed and the snake finally slithered slowly, nursing wounds, into the grasses from where he had come. That night, under a canopy of stars, the two didn't sleep at all. But as the sun rose over the horizon they were lulled to rest by the sound of a turtle singing from the shore.

. . .

The goose missed Elizabeth that morning as the crone sat on her nest watching the activities below. It was fortunate the goose did miss what was going on because Hal was riding his large tractor over the newly formed sprouts of grass. She would have also seen the bucket (head of the turtle) on the end of what she would have described as the turtle's neck pushing the dock (platform) into the water. And she would have seen the nest (her nest) rocking back and forth with the force.

As the sound of the tractor died, the goose woke and looked toward shore. She saw the sage riding out toward her nesting site, tie up his floater (boat), and pull two long necks and heads (anchors) from the water. She saw him ride the nest, by extending his wing into the water, back to shore with the floater behind. As he joined the crone on her nest, she knew all was right with the world for he had come back to protect the crone.

# Chapter 4

Elizabeth was home from the hospital. Little did she know the goose had taken a mate, built her nest, and laid her eggs. Elizabeth's world had temporarily stopped because of her leg; she had forgotten there were other life events taking place around her of equal importance, she had temporarily reverted to the east.

Gwen was providing her with meals every couple of days or so. Then, of course, there was Della who came down almost every day 'for a chat'. Elizabeth was worn out after these "chats" and after three days she had to find a way to tell Della that she didn't need quite that much company. Perhaps she could suggest calling her on the days that Gwen didn't come down. She would tell her a little white lie and say it was only two days a week when Gwen didn't come by. Or she could mention her poetry and how she was thankful for the other uninterrupted days to write. Of course this might not work because Della would know when Gwen was visiting. Della knew everything! What a dilemma!

The hospital had given her crutches and she needed to become proficient as soon as possible; there were chores waiting. Everyday she walked around the cabin. Since it was only 24 x 28 feet there wasn't much space on the first floor. Of course the porch provided a little extra room to walk at 10 x12 feet. She couldn't wait to go up and down the stairs. The doctor, however, said this wouldn't happen until she had a walking cast. She was a prisoner in her own home! She was so thankful the weather had taken a turn and she could almost count on 50+ to 60 degree days. These gave her a chance to go out on her deck to write.

· · ·

"Anybody home?"

Elizabeth called back, a bit rudely, "Of course, where did you think I would go?"

"It's Della, Elizabeth," Della replied in her ear piercing voice.

"I didn't expect you." So why did you come, she wanted to add.

"Well, I knows you were by yourself. Gwen said she wasn't coming today. I ran into her in the grocery store, that's how I knows."

"Well, don't just stand there, come in and have a seat."

"Don't mind if I do. I'll just get a cold Coke out of the refrigerator. You do have Coke?" Della asked as she already had the door half open. "Would you like me to bring you anything, Elizabeth?"

"No, I have some hot tea already, but thanks for asking."

"I seen Millie today. She's got bladder problems. Can't stop peeing. Every time she gets up it runs down her leg. She doesn't even know she has to go. Guess she's going to some specialist to get some kind of test. They put those tubes in her, one all the way up to her bladder and one in her rear. Then they put those little round things, like they put on your heart to test it, on her rear too. Then they fill her with water till she can't stand it and let her pee it all out. Sounds pretty bad if you ask me. I sure wouldn't want them messing with my 'pee-er' and rear end like that, would you?"

"No, it sounds..."

"I guess they can do that to men too. Millie told me that her son had to have it done too but they had to put it in his thing instead. My Mike would never have stood for that, God rests his soul. John has had to work overtime all these past two weeks. His job is gearing up for making some more iron. Seems as if there is more of a demand since Bush put through that new law. Guess they are going to have to hire more guys. John may even get a promotion."

"Speaking of John," Elizabeth said as Della took a drink of her Coke finally, "do you think he could come down and cut my lawn and do some other chores when the time comes? I don't want it to get too long while I am laid up and it will be needing to be cut soon. I'll pay him, of course."

"Sure he will. Anything else you need to have done? "

"No, I think the rest can wait until I get a walking cast. I don't think that will be too long. I have an appointment with the doctor in two weeks."

"Did I tell you Suzy went to the doctor the other day and she's pregnant? Her boyfriend doesn't want to get married though. What kind of a man would not do the right thing? Suzy says it is okay by her. I just don't understand these young'ins. Of course they say the apple doesn't fall far from the tree. Look at her mother shacking up with that married man! I just don't know what kinda girl we raised. Thank God for Carol though. She's turned out good but that husband of hers is still too uppity for my liking. But I love my grandsons anyways. Seeings they look like their mother and all."

"Well, Della, we were once kids too, and did a few things our parents probably didn't approve of."

"Did I ever tell you the story of how Mike and I were childhood sweethearts?" Of course she had told Elizabeth at least a dozen times, but Elizabeth was too polite to say anything. "Well, right on the front lawn of our school he asked me to marry him. I still got the leaf from the tree where we were standing when he asked. Just as sweet as all get out. Why yes. He says to me, 'Della will you take this poor farm boy to marry you?' Then he says to me, I've signed up for the army. Goin' in next week.' Well, I didn't know whether to be happy or not. But I knews he was doing the right thing. Then alls the time he was in the war I would get these sweet love letters. And whens he comes back we marched down the aisle a week later. Good thing, too, because nine months to the day Judy come along. I sure do miss him. Say, how'd you and Carl get together? I knows you had no kids. How come? Do you miss him as much as I miss my Mickey?"

Elizabeth was trying to figure out an answer to these personal questions she knew were coming, as they came every time Della got onto this topic. "Carl and I met in college. He was a history major and I was getting my teaching degree. We met in the library and dated on and off until the end of college. He couldn't go into the army due to his failing eyesight. Since the degenerating eyesight, I mean failing eyesight, could be hereditary or might be passed on to our children, we decided it would be best not to have any. Yes, I do miss him so." Elizabeth had a tear in her eye. Unusual as this was, she never cried in front of anyone except her best friend Sarah, she tried to cover it up by yawning.

"I can sees I plumb wore you out. I shouldn't have stayed so long. John will be home in an hour or so and expect his dinner. I needs to get going. I'll call you in a day or so and we can have another short chat."

"That would be nice," Elizabeth lied.

"So long Elizabeth. Hope that leg starts feeling better soon. I'll ask John about the mowing and other chores but I don't sees why he wouldn't do it."

"Bye, Della."

Elizabeth took a big sigh when she was gone. She was exhausted after all.

. . .

There was a knock on the door the following day around 11:30 and Elizabeth got her crutches to answer it. It was Gwen bringing her something to eat. Unlike Della, Gwen had some manners and waited to be asked inside.

"Hi, Gwen, come in. I see you brought something to eat again, delicious no doubt."

"Oh, I just brought some club sandwiches, raw vegetables, dip, and a surprise dessert for lunch. I thought you could use a little break from the hot dish regimen."

"I'm glad you came today. It has been a little quiet this morning. I've been sitting with my leg up and reading this book and my eyes are quite tired. Have you ever read <u>Women on The Edge of Time</u>, by Marge Piercy? It was published in the 70's."

"No, but I like her work."

"Well, you can borrow it when I'm finished. But here I am engaging you in conversation when I should be setting a table fit for these fine treats."

"Here, let me do it, you should probably stay off the leg. If I know you, you are on it more than the doctor said was good for healing?" Gwen smiled. "Where are the dishes and silverware?"

"The dishes are in the cabinets facing the refrigerator, the silverware is in the drawer next to it, and the glasses are above the drawer on the other side of that same cabinet. Thanks."

While Gwen was getting all the dishes, Elizabeth put the place mats on the table. She was so glad she had turned the porch into a four season one so they could enjoy a full view of the lake while eating.

"I think I found them all."

"There's a tray in the lower cabinet by the sink. Use that to carry them out here."

"What tasty sandwiches," Elizabeth commented as she sunk her teeth into a ham, cheese, pickle, lettuce, and tomato club. "And the vegetables are so fresh. Where did you get them?"

"Thank you. I got them at Jim's. Today is Wednesday and he always gets a fresh shipment in. That's when I try to do my shopping."

"I didn't know that."

"What a beautiful day today is. I would have walked over but this load was too much. It seems a shame to drive such a short distance."

"Isn't the view beautiful? The shadows from the trees looked a deep true blue this morning as they danced across the leftover snow. I think we have seen the last snowfall this year, though. The geese have been continuing their flights north. I would say that pretty much indicates a thaw farther north."

"Yes, and the lake is so clear right now. I noticed the increased activity, too. I was also watching the ganders vying for the goose's attention. They now have a nest somewhere. I am sure they are taking care of their eggs."

"Oh my, I have forgotten the goose. I must get out and keep an eye out for them. You say she has a family? Do you know the whereabouts? I was just glad to be home and forgot this was mating season. How could I possibly do that? I guess it is time to get out my pen and paper for another writing session and capture the beauty of the geese."

"I don't know how you do that; just sit down and write," Gwen added.

"It's not as easy as it looks. The final poem may look very little like the original one when I get done editing. Then again it may be perfect right from the start," Elizabeth laughed.

"I'm not sure where the nest is located. Maybe you and Hal can go on a trip around the lake in search of them. I'm sure he would like that. That is... when you feel up to it. Would you like your dessert now?"

"Oh my, yes. Should we have some hot tea to go with it?"

"That would be great. I'll put the kettle on. Where's your tea?"

"In the only cupboard you haven't looked in yet." They both laughed.

Elizabeth gazed out the windows toward the lake as Gwen prepared the tea and dessert. She was inspired and knew she would have to write right after Gwen had left.

"Here's a nice hot cup of tea and a piece of Johnny cake with honey."

"I can't tell you how long it has been since I've had Johnny cake," Elizabeth smiled and said as she took her first bite. "Mmm, it is very good. Just the right amount of sweetness. You are such a good cook, Gwen."

"Oh, you always say that."

The two women relaxed and enjoyed the view and cake together. "It was so nice to be able to have a friend you could sit and say nothing to," Elizabeth and Gwen both reflected privately on the moment.

"I've let time get away from me," Gwen said as she looked at her watch, breaking the silence. "Hal will be home soon and we are going to a movie at 4:30 and then have a late dinner. We just love having that new theater in Guterson. I had better be going. I'll just put the leftovers in the refrigerator, okay?"

"That's fine. It has been a lovely afternoon."

"Thanks for coming by," Elizabeth called after her as Gwen shut the door.

• • •

The mood to write passed and she decided to take a walk. Elizabeth was so happy to be off that deck. Even though she loved sitting in her Adirondack chair, all day long had gotten to be a bit too much. Elizabeth was never fond of following rules and even though she still had her first cast on, and would for another week, she went down the stairs and across the lawn on her crutches, moving like a goose.

"Oh, wouldn't my friends have a heart attack if they knew what I was doing now!" Elizabeth laughed out loud as the birds listened to her song.

The original cast would be removed after five weeks, counting the week she was in the hospital, and she would get her walking cast this week. They had told her that one would then be on about three weeks to a month before she would be completely healed. How would she ever get to the chores she needed to do in the next three or four weeks? Was John available? Della hadn't phoned back after their conversation the other day. Then she remembered the gifts of the East and her poem, written when she couldn't move around. It helped calm her thoughts and renew her spirit as she made her way through the little snow that was left.

Gifts of the East

Embark on journeys

one step, two steps,

in the East.

Present moment is ours.

Scenic butterfly absorbed us.

When young it was instinctive,

a bubble of awareness.

Not inside, not outside,

not far away, in the present.


Accomplish physical

tasks around you.

Watch senses,

watch self-giving,

watch self-actions,

in acquisition

the excellence of healing arts.

Passage, first stage,

develop power of human will.

-Elizabeth Washburn

These were the lessons Elizabeth now drew on. She went back over the events in her mind as she walked carefully, with her crutches, along the shore. She had felt old when she was in the hospital, and sorry for herself. The lessons of the East had to be revisited on the journey of life. They grounded her to her beginnings, as if in sync, in spring, with everything beginning to live again; the birds laying eggs or the geese having goslings. Each of the birds lived in the present and so must she. The past was that. There was no room for what ifs; trials were. What if she hadn't worked so long that day? What if she hadn't been so tired she didn't retie her boot lace? What if she had put on more clothing? What if the stairs had not had spaces to catch a toe in? What if...?

There was no room to look toward the future either. What will happen when her cast is off? What will happen when the deer came to eat her plants? What will happen when it is time to plant? What will happen when it is time to remove the leaves? What will happen when she has to cut the grass? What will happen when...? Elizabeth must live in the present. She had no problem accomplishing that now.

Elizabeth had gathered her seeds for many years. She was a master gardener and the beauty of her friendships proved it. Everyday, while she was on crutches, her faithful friends would bring food or come to chat. When she needed to go the long distance to the doctor there was always a friend at her doorstep to take her there. Even the goose kept a watchful eye while she kept one on her. So Elizabeth learned to take one day at a time and not worry about what she should have done, or would do, to make her condition better. The day ended in total peace.

# Chapter 5

As Elizabeth watched Sarah's taillights disappear she felt the same peace as she had last spring. How could so few words mean so much?

• • •

"Another new day," she sang delightfully to the earth as the sun was set to rise and the smell of the damp air brought the hint of a left over winter in the memory. Spring, however, had finally taken hold and the air was literally singing.

She got her binoculars and notebook and was determined to observe the goose and her gander. She knew that first she would have to locate them so she made sure she was up early. She was so glad to have a day free of visitors and workers.

By first light, dressed warmly in blue jeans with one seam split to her thigh then pinned together, a long-sleeved flannel shirt and her black and red wool shirt over it, for these were cool spring mornings, Elizabeth took up a position on her deck. She couldn't use her porch due to its limited view of the west side of the lake. She wasn't sure where to find the goose and wanted a wide-angle view.

About fifteen minutes after the sun could be seen on the horizon, Elizabeth saw movement on the northwestern side of the glasslike, deep, reflecting lake. It was very slight, maybe just the water itself (she saw this a lot when fishing), so she retrieved her binoculars from the arm of the chair. It was too dark to tell clearly what she was looking at. She kept watching. Soon the figure turned into a goose as the sun rose in the sky and a white band held the goose chin high. Was it her goose? Elizabeth knew that there would be at least one or two other families nesting on the lake; they had been there for many years. Fortunately, she was fairly aware of where their nests had been and began to look for them to be sure they were still there. She spotted one goose swimming on the east side of the large island. That took care of that family. The next one would be harder to spot since it had always made its nest on the beaver house, almost due west from where she sat. She became worried because she didn't see the beaver dam. Then she remembered that Hal and a couple of other guys had destroyed it last fall after having trapped it out. Then she saw the other set of geese. They must have their nest tucked back into the little cove. So there were three families and she had spotted the right one first, the family of her goose was on the northwest side. She knew there would be no more because the south side lacked the vegetation needed for shelter and food.

Elizabeth looked back to where she saw the first goose but it was no longer there. Elizabeth began to widen her search until she had a circle with the center the island and a radius of about fifty feet, or as nearly as she could estimate from her distance. There was, however, no goose to be found. She had missed her opportunity today. She would have to use all of her concentration tomorrow (a gift of the East), to not think about the past geese families and only focus on the one she concerned herself with at present.

· · ·

On the Monday of the last week of April, John came to help with the chores Elizabeth could not yet do.

"Elizabeth, you around?"

"Yes. Come in, John," she called back, from the porch.

"Did my Mom call you?"

"Yes, she did, and said you would be down today."

"Well, I have today off. It's part of my vacation. I'll be going on a trip to North and South Dakota tomorrow. I'll try to get as much done as I can today."

"Thank you for coming. I know how important your vacation time is to you. Are you going to the Black Hills?"

"Yeah," he said, letting his manners slip. "So what do you need to have done?"

"The most important chores are to get the leaves up and the window wells removed. They are long overdue."

"Okay. So where's your mower and bagger?"

"They are in the pole barn and I'm afraid you will have to put the bagger on before you start."

"No problem."

"Then here are the keys to the pole barn and the tractor."

As John proceeded to get the equipment from the pole barn, Elizabeth returned to her tea and roll. Della had sent some sticky buns down with John, and she'd had just enough room for one more cup of tea to have with them. Elizabeth was so thankful for her friends. John had had learning problems when he was younger and could only find minimum wage work, so whenever she had chores she couldn't do herself, she always called to see if he was available. Of course, this year there were going to be many more than usual.

Today was going to be unusually hot for this time of the year. The average temperatures were in the 60's but it was going to be 73 degrees today. This was not a good sign. She felt sorry for John but was consoled by the fact that he was still a young man.

Elizabeth held her pen in her left hand and her notebook was on her lap tray. Sitting on the deck today was a luxury. There was never a day that she could remember when someone else did the work and she could relax.

Waiting

Elusive feather floats.

Feel the gentle breath.

As it rides sine-curved currents.

Catch the warm, descending plume.

-Elizabeth Washburn

Lake

I sit on an Adirondack chair,

on a deck,

with my t-shirt's sleeves

rolled, so the sun,

trying to break the clouds

will toast me evenly.

I have discarded my over shirt,

and I wear shorts,

exposing my wrinkled limbs

to the warmth of the orb.

And now I drift off to nap

feeling freedom.

It's red singing hot at

four o'clock,

not so this morning.

"The crowd was standing

close."

I do not know where

my words come from.

The horse fly keeps trying

to bite,

must be rain coming.

I rise from the Adirondack chair.

-Elizabeth Washburn

Elizabeth had just finished her last poem and could see she was quite red when John came up the deck steps. She saw that the bagging had been finished.

"Just got your window wells taken off. They are piled in the back yard. Where would you like them?"

"I usually take them down below. There is a large bin outside the basement where I store them. It's getting late though, are you sure you can finish?"

"No problem."

As he finished up the chores, Elizabeth went to put some aloe on her arms and legs. Her tender skin was especially red. She then went out back and walked around the property. John had done a marvelous job and she would reward him with an extra $20 for his efforts.

When he finished, he found her and they walked back up to the house. She offered him another Coke before he left and wrote out a generous check for his days work.

"Thank you."

"You're welcome. Enjoy your trip, and tell your mother the sticky buns were very good."

"Looks like a storm's coming. Could be a bad one," John said, as he got into his truck and left.

Elizabeth looked to the southwest and noticed the clouds gathering. She wondered why she had not noticed it sooner. She had forgotten about her poem.

# Chapter 6

Was the internal clock of the goose responsible or was it purely instincts that accounted for the goose's actions, as her sense of timing seemed to coincide with the cycle of the Medicine Wheel, just as Elizabeth's did? She was young and certainly acted out of the eastern gifts. She lived in the present. When she had laid her eggs and they were incubating, all her time seemed to be spent nursing them to goslings. There were the times she had to stand and turn her eggs so they were evenly developed. She took great care to hide herself from the predators, which the gander alerted her to. Never moving her body, she blended in with her surroundings. In the early morning and evening she took great care not to swim too far away lest a fox or some other predator were to steal an egg. Instinctively she knew the radius within which she could swim.

The goose did not live in the past. What if she had flown South? What if there had been no crone last winter? What if she had not found a mate? These were of no concern. There was only learning how to have a family and teaching her goslings to swim and fly. She believed in the unseen. She trusted her ancestors. She was devoted to her life in the present.

The goose did not live in the future either. When would her eggs hatch? When would the goslings learn to swim? When would her family fly south? She focused her attention on the present. She watched over all her eggs. She was innocent of all the trials a goose must face in raising her family. The innocence of a mouse living in a bubble, in the present, safe from the future, not troubled by the past.

In the early mornings the goose was full of joy because of the wonderful nest and because of the wonderful gander that were part of her life. She trusted her mate and, with great courage, left her nest to walk to the water. Most days, as the light in the sky was coming over the horizon, she drank and ate fully of the many grasses that had been provided. Then she would preen herself and splash and be filled with pure joy as the colors broke through the marine-blue colored sky. As she gained even more courage she would swim further from her nest and enjoy the freshness of each given day.

That day started off like any other day. Her days had become so routine she could have lived them in her sleep. She swam and preened then went back to her nest to continue incubating her eggs. She gave them all a turn before settling her puffed out body down. It was time for the game. The goose had decided if the crone was going to watch her constantly, with those bulging eyes, she should keep an eye on her too. So, with one part of her mind on motherhood and one on the crone's antics, her day began.

This was a game and she enjoyed playing it because it broke the monotony of just sitting on the nest, performing her daily duties and returning to her nest as soon as she could from her swims. As predicted, the crone's eyes began to bulge and she used her wings to hold them in. She moved them up and down and in and out. The goose lay very still so she would have the advantage and watch the crone watch her.

Then, as if the Great Spirit had said enough is enough, her attention was brought back to the nest. Something stirred beneath her. At first the goose went on alert and immediately her attention to the crone became a distant second. "The bull snake has found its way into the nest!" she cried out to the gander. The gander, however, had not sounded off. It must be something different.

A tickle came. Then a few more. Then there were several nudges on her underside. The goose slowly stood and at once began sounding her chant. The birds stopped to listen. Elizabeth stopped and stared directly at the nest. "The eggs are hatching," the goose announced. She had become a mother. How proud her gander would be.

One by one the goslings, five in all, broke the grayish egg shell. Then all at once they began climbing out of the nest barely able to get their little heads on its edge before boosting themselves upward. The fuzzy, mustard-colored seeds began walking.

Immediately a straight line was formed with the goose in front, the little goslings, and the gander in back. They paraded proudly around searching for food. They didn't venture too far from the nest, though, when they began to eat. The goose knew they would be eating for a long time because her goslings would eat almost continuously right from the very start of their lives; the stories had been told.

It seemed like they had been feeding forever when the gander started hissing. The goose and her brood scurried back to the safety of her nest to wait out the results. Fortunately for them it was nothing more than an angler's boat coming a little too close to the island for their comfort.

As soon as the danger was over, out of the nest the goslings went again and ate for what seemed like an eternity.

· · ·

Budding Color

Life, mustard-colored.

Moving as family now.

Eat with no caring.

-Elizabeth Washburn

Haiku was one of her favorite forms of poetry and Elizabeth, having been witness to the new life, was compelled to write a poem immediately.

· · ·

Without missing a beat, the next day the goose led the goslings to the waters edge. Within twenty-four hours they swam with the goose and the gander, and as they swam the crone and the sage moved across the water under the goose's ever watchful eye.

The crone was on a funny looking floater with the sage using his wings to guide it. The floater was as large as a tree, or so it appeared, and three times the size that her platform had been. There was a large upside-down nest covering the crone and sage on the platform. She had wondered what the sage was doing at the crone's with such a funny looking floater. Now she knew. They were floating across the lake.

At first the goose had seen the sage helping the crone on top of it, just as she use to get on her platform. She noticed the crone had her bulging eyes drooped on her chest, a long stem on one wing, and a little black object on the other. They had then begun to float away from the long platform. Soon she had seen them heading straight for her family. Her gander also had seen it and began to keep a keen eye out lest the floater got too close to their nest.

Then, before the geese even knew it, the floater seemed to be within wings reach. The gander swam out to meet it and attacked while the goose and goslings scrambled back to shore and ran for the nest. The floater settled in not twenty feet away and stopped moving. The pecking, batting of wings, and hissing had little or no affect on the crone or the sage or their floater, so the gander went back to protect his family. He vowed he would do them harm if they should come any closer.

As the floater sat unmoving, the crone took the stick and placed the small black box on top of it. She looked into the box with one eye; the goose saw it was not bulging anymore. A small click barely sounded. To the geese, though, it had seemed like a shot from a gun. This had been followed by several more and the goose stood stunned, waiting to feel the impact. Then, just as silently as it had come, the floater began to move away. It had only repositioned itself; the goose couldn't help but look up from her still position. Bang, bang, bang it sounded before she could resume her unmoving body position. What was it the crone was doing? Why had she been looking at her with such funny looking things and shooting at her with a small black box? The goose wondered why she hadn't fallen like the stories of old told?

Then the noise stopped and, just like that, the floater silently began to move farther away. It went back to the crone's long platform. The crone got off and, with the sage still on-board, it floated away down the lake.

• • •

That evening, while the goose was brooding, both geese felt a change in the atmosphere. At first the change was subtle; the blackening sky coming before the sun had set, and then the air became heavy. The goose cut her evening swim short and headed back to her nest. The rains started. This was not weather they had seen before and it felt like all the predators were closing in. Suddenly the sky lit up with one striking bolt of blue light. A sound of great proportions was heard. She fluffed her body and bore her head into the nest to protect her brood. As the water rose on the lake, she wondered what evils the birth of her goslings had brought and whether they would have a nest come morning light.

# Chapter 7

As Elizabeth looked at the three framed photographs, she listened to the news. Her mind had been wandering. She tried to put out of her mind the suffering she felt from her sunburn. How foolish she had been. The newscaster's voice caught her attention. She focused on the present.

"There is a severe thunderstorm warning out for all of Jackson, Candigo, Oak, and Wyngate counties until 2 am this morning. There is a possibility of large hail and tornadoes accompanying these storms. They have already moved through eastern Minnesota and are expected in Western Wisconsin around 10 o'clock tonight. Be sure to stay tuned for any further developments."

Elizabeth became concerned. She set about gathering candles from various locations, matches, and a flashlight. She put fresh batteries into the radio just in case. She always found it difficult to sleep through bad storms even though she had a futon, just for such occasions, in the basement. Then Elizabeth fixed her dinner and curled up with her book. She knew something had to give in the atmosphere today, due to the above average temperatures.

The first rain started about 10:30. The thunder crashed after the sky brightened from intense lightening bolts. Using the "second rule" to determine how far away the eye of the storm was, she counted to herself; Elizabeth determined the storm was still quite far off. Elizabeth had always enjoyed the beginnings of a storm, though, and put on a rain proof jacket and hat and went outside to enjoy the distant show. Sooner than she had anticipated, it began to rain harder. She went inside and picked up her book again but got little reading done as she began to get nervous.

Then hail began to pound the roof. The wind spit the hail against the side of the house and windows. Hoping it would not be large enough to bust a window, she looked out. An enormous crash of thunder boomed directly overhead, the lights went out and Elizabeth was left standing by the window without a light. Lightening must have hit a power line.

Elizabeth grabbed the flashlight from the table close by and began lighting candles. Soon the room had a soft glow to it; when it wasn't lighting up like a Roman Candle from the lightening outside. The lightening had produced eerie shadows extending from the base of the trees. The winds had picked up force and for the first time Elizabeth realized the severity of the storm she was in; once again, all alone. The radio was playing softly at her side so she turned it up louder. Through the crackling sound she barely heard the news she dreaded most.

"There have been tornado sightings in Oak county. Anyone in the path should seek shelter immediately. As of yet none has been reported on the ground but these storms can turn deadly at any moment."

That was all that she needed. She blew out the candles. Taking three with her and, picking up her flashlight and radio, Elizabeth headed to her basement to sit out the storm. She prayed this storm would leave her trees standing.

• • •

Elizabeth surveyed her property the next morning, noting little damage. There were some large branches and many small ones to navigate over, but generally the land looked untouched. She would get someone to help her pick them up in a day or two. She thanked her totem and the Great Spirit for diverting the tornadoes and golf ball size hail to her south, but also said a bit of a prayer for those people who took the brunt of the storm.

A smile began to form around Elizabeth's mouth just then, as she noticed some wildflowers were making their debut. Out of the beast arose beauty. Those of a blue shade, like the violet Sunbonnet of the southwest, would be needed for the May Day ritual. April had seemed like such a long month, and ending with that storm last night had not helped. She reached down to scratch an itch she couldn't get to because of the walking cast.

. . .

The following Sunday, after worshiping the almighty coffee cup, Hal picked up branches and Elizabeth picked the lovely blue wildflowers.

It was a perfect day, with temperatures in the low-sixties, on which she performed the May Day ritual of the crone

Sacred Birth

The child born with the morning sun,

black turning into all colors, all brothers

between earth and air grows the seed,

potential for physical, emotional, mental,

spiritual; turning into blues of the sky.

Receiving nourishment, protection,

roots, limbs growing into four directions,

wholeness of perfection.

-Elizabeth Washburn

The Ritual of Affirmation was best performed in full sunlight out-of-doors. She prepared an altar with two deep blue candles upon a cloth of paler blue. The flowers were strewn about its top. There was also a potion of violets which was strained into a clear glass with two spoonfuls of honey. She had various shades of blue and ornaments of gold, silver and crystal.

As Elizabeth lit the candles, she began with the words: "Sprung from DARK into LIGHT, FLAMES of BLUE. Most INNOCENT and INTENSE, Released from DEPTHS of NIGHT, LEACHED from PALE BONES of WINTER, the MATRIX of EARTH, RISEN in FIRES of SUN, fed by WATERS of SPRING. Now they BURN, now ASCEND as WINGS of BLUE FLAME, ASPIRING to AZURE REALM to where FLESH ASPIRES, GROWTH shall find PERFECT FORM..."

The ritual continued with a passage speaking of the balance between heaven and earth. Then, as the potion was held up, there were many words about the blending of earth and sky, with feet taking root upon the earth in harmony with the flowers and the trees. Elizabeth then made a wreath of the flowers and stems and took one violet in her hand. She would carefully preserve the violet, for its powers shall not pass away.

Then she danced the celebration of life.

# Chapter 8

As the day broke, the geese remained where they had lain down the previous night. The waves and the water had not invaded their nest. The furry brood stirred beneath the goose's down covered body and the gander sang praises to his mate. He was so proud to have found a goose so intelligent as to pick such a safe and protected site. He had been sure the water would sweep his family away, as its fierce tongue lapped at the grass all around. However, the goose had hunkered down and protected the family from harm. He sang her a song bringing the lake residents out of their homes to listen.

The goose let the mustard seeds come out one by one. Rejoicing they were all there, the goose led them to the water, with each one following the one in front of it, as the gander brought up the rear. The brood could swim but needed constant reminders to stay with their parents. It doesn't take long for the more adventurous to want to strike out on their own. They swam to the east and around the island. They were proud to show off their skills to the other family. They stopped at the large island to have their first eating fest of the day. They swam to the far shores in search of tender morsels of new shoots.

As they approached the bank of the crone's side they saw an unusual event taking place. Wanting to protect their family, the geese did not go on shore but swam back and forth observing and drinking and pretending to eat. What was this crone doing? She had one big foot and one small one. Even with this bulging foot, though, the crone seemed to move as she always did. "How odd," the goose quizzically communicated to the gander. She had a long platform with long skinny legs and tiny feet in front of her. It didn't seem to move, like all the crone's other platforms. The others only moved, when the sage was there riding the large turtle or on a floater. He wasn't here today, so maybe that was why the it remained still. She was placing different sorts of shoots and seeds on it as well as objects the geese had no familiarity with. All of a sudden, the crone began making noise unlike any the geese had ever heard. Her songs hurt their ears and they moved farther away, just to be safe.

Soon she was doing a dance while her feathers were flying around her. Seeing no sage, the goose wondered for whom she did her dance. She must have carried on for what would have been two feedings, and her goslings were getting hungry. Just as they were about to swim to another location, the crone came to a halt, almost as if she were treading air. Both her feet then began to move slowly around the platform.

They saw her gather all the seeds left on the platform into a small brown nest which hung from her wing. She took the platform's top layer and, using her wings, made it almost disappear. This she placed in the nest, too. Then the oddest thing happened. She took the platform and bent its legs and feet, making them disappear. She dragged it to her nest on the hill with the small nest still hanging from her wing.

Feeling brave after last night's storm, the geese went on shore to eat after the crone went into her nest. They hoped she would not repeat her performance. After all, these were the best shoots on the lake. Just to be safe, all the while the goose kept a mindful eye out toward the crone's nest before leading her family home.

. . .

Day in and day out, the brood grew as they paid mind to their business, just as Elizabeth paid mind to her business of gathering flowers. Their life became a ritual of swimming and eating. They had to show off to the other families every day and began to notice there were other goslings on the lake, too. One day, while swimming, they formed a society with the other families on the lake.

It became quite large when all the young and older geese were swimming together, but as each family joined they increased their circle of safety. Eventually the circles coincided in the middle of the larger encompassing circle. As they met, the geese swam around and around each other, getting ever closer, then pulling away. Finally, some of the young goslings went right up and introduced themselves. They had found other brothers and sisters to play with. Soon one parent took up the lead and the other goslings fell into line with a gander at the rear.

The other geese were left, for the first time, with some quality time for themselves. Off went the rest in a grand day parade around the lake. This happened over and over all day long, between feedings, with different parents taking charge. As nightfall came, each family claimed their goslings and swam back to their nesting area. Not being able to count, the goose never noticed she was missing one of her goslings as they settled down for the night. As was often the case, another family would adopt another family's young. The goose and gander had never experienced this, being new parents and all.

The next morning when the sun rose and called to them to take their early morning swim, the goose and gander noticed they seemed to have fewer youngsters than the day before. There was a loud honking heard all around the lake. It was so loud that Elizabeth and Hal and Gwen had to go outside to see what the ruckus was all about.

Elizabeth could not tell, so she went to get her binoculars. She looked across the lake. The goose was looking straight back at her. Then an alarming thing began to happen. The gander came as fast as he could to Elizabeth's side of the lake, and began what looked like a search. Turning her attention back to the island, Elizabeth saw the goose and only four goslings. Where was the fifth one? Was this what all the fuss was about? Did they think she had been responsible for its disappearance? The goose was desperately searching the island while the gander was searching the shore.

Elizabeth went to get her tripod and camera. She set it up on the deck to document this event. She photographed the gander's desperate search and the goose watching the other four very carefully. Soon the gander seemed to give up. He went back to the island and the family proceeded to swim out from there, across the lake, and join up with the other families. The goose and gander did not know their fifth gosling was part of one of the other families, but the older geese comforted them and told them that this is what sometimes happens and, no matter where the gosling was, it would still be brought up correctly.

# Chapter 9

Hal had the day off at the end of the week and took Elizabeth to the doctor to have her walking cast removed. The doctor examined the leg after removing the cast and declared her healed and as good as new. Elizabeth bent down to feel her foot and then lifted her leg in the air. She got up, walked around, and proclaimed how it felt wonderful to walk on air. She swore she would never work until she was too tired to hold her head up again, no matter how much she thought she needed to finish.

"So, Elizabeth, is there anywheres else you want to go before I take you home?"

"Yes, there is. It is May and, because the weather has been so nice lately, I thought I would get my flowers to plant in all my gardens. Some of them should have been planted right after the frost went out of the ground, but it hasn't been that long so I think I'm okay."

"So be it then," answered Hal with the tone of a man who hates to shop. He knew what it was like to take Gwen flower shopping and he almost always begged off. But this was Elizabeth and he had asked. They got into his truck and headed off down the road.

"Are you sure you want to do this for me Hal?"

"Anything you want, that's why I asked. Here's Carl's Nursery now."

Quickly departing the vehicle, Elizabeth began her shopping, periodically asking Hal for his opinion.

Elizabeth had four annual gardens, that also contained some perennial flowers, and her rock-forest garden setting. She needed to keep as busy in the spring and summer months as she did the rest of the year. She wasn't about to sit around any time in the near future if she could help it at all. Elizabeth was sure she had calluses in new places from all those weeks of doing nothing. Just the immobility of the past two months had been enough to dampen her otherwise happy mood. So off she went with two shopping carts. Elizabeth pushing one and Hal pushing the other.

"Let me see, I'll start with my lake garden. It needs a wide border. I'll get some flowering cabbage in shades of green. Green is always nice next to the lake, don't you think Hal? There is also some Creeping Phlox in there that I have to thin out so I must get something else that will blend with the green; blue, Morning Glory blue. A couple more should do. Something a little brighter. Ahh, some golden Marigolds and red Poppies. Oh, maybe I'll put in some Snapdragons, too. That takes care of the lake garden."

By this time her cart was half full and Hal could see two carts would never be enough for the number of flowers she was buying. When would she have time to do all of this anyway? Elizabeth was at the table of Forget-Me-Nots. She bought two trays of intense blue ones. She also bought two trays of white Alyssum.

"Come on Hal, I need your cart. Mine is full. Let's go get us some red and rich deep blue Sage," Elizabeth said with a twinkle in her eye, knowing full well he was already tiring of this foolish behavior of an old woman.

"Now for my butterfly garden. Do you remember when I had all those oak and pine trees thinned out this past fall? Well, I decided to put a butterfly garden in that clearing so I could watch them from the deck. Some of the flowers will also attract the humming birds. It's the only way I can attract them back and not have to worry about the bears wrecking the feeders."

Hal had not seen her this happy since before she broke her leg. He also didn't think he had ever heard her talk so much and so fast. Women always amazed him.

"I'm going to get blue Pansies over here and some bicolored Petunias over there. Come on, let's get the Verbena in purple, too. Hal, be a gem and get another cart." He had already taken steps to the front of the store to get one while pushing his full cart, which he would leave under surprised eyes.

Elizabeth waited impatiently and was just about to go find him when he returned.

" I lefts the other cart with the check out lady. Where-?" Before he could finish his question she was off again.

"Over here. I'm going to get some red Zinnias and yellow Sunflowers. Don't you think that will be nice for the butterflies too?"

"Yeah," Hal mumbled, knowing she wasn't really asking him the question anyway.

"And here are the Impatiens for the rock garden. I need another cart because I want corals, reds, lavenders and…that's it."

Hal got the other cart, leaving his as he did the last time, and came back for the Impatiens.

"Do you need help out?" asked the sales clerk.

"Yes," answered a weary Hal. "It's the red truck over here," Hal pointed as they made their way across the parking lot.

They loaded the truck and, after two hours of shopping, were on their way.

"I will get out my garden tools tomorrow and start preparing the beds. We sure could use some gentle rains to soften up the earth; downpours like the other night do no good, they just muddy everything up," Elizabeth commented, laughing at her own joke. "Hal, you are a wonderful man to do this for me. Sunday is Mother's Day you know, and the beds need to be ready by then."

Hal helped Elizabeth line up the boxes of plants along the house, next to the hose. Then he was on his way.

• • •

Elizabeth went into the house, but stayed only long enough to get her tripod and camera, and her various array of lenses. She still contended that a SLR was better than a digital camera for taking wildlife photographs. She went down to the swing and set up the equipment in a partially hidden area, with a clear view of the islands. She focused on the peninsula where she had seen the goose had her nest. She knew that the brood would grow fast, and wanted to document their life as well as she could.

Since they were already on Daylight Saving Time, Elizabeth could get some quality pictures with good light this evening. She sat on the swing, with her binoculars at her side, thinking about her childhood and her favorite poem by Robert Louis Stevenson, The Swing.

Periodically she would take up her binoculars and look toward the island in search of her goose and family. Just about 6:30, Elizabeth saw movement. She picked up her binoculars and saw it, the family she had been hunting for all day. Knowing her time was limited, she went to the camera. Every time the family came within her viewing field, which was set on wide angle, she took a photograph. Click, click went the shutter. She had it on automatic wind so she could take them in rapid succession. They swam, dipped, drank and the older ones preened. The younger brood was allowed to swim on their own, not in a straight line, while they were enjoying their evening out.

As the sun began to turn the sky into hues of rainbow colors, the geese made their way back to their nesting site. Elizabeth gathered her equipment and went up the trail to the house. One by one the stars came out, but the loveliest star, not a star at all, was the planet Venus. The moon looked like the end of a thumbnail.

# Chapter 10

Elizabeth went inside from her morning swim and dressed in her faded blue jeans, a long sleeve T-shirt, and a green sweatshirt which she knew would not stay on long today if she had to work in the sun. The weather man had promised the high 60's, maybe even 70, today. She put on a pair of waterproof shoes and put her gardening gloves in her pocket.

Taking her keys out of her other pocket, Elizabeth opened the pole barn door. Her eyes twinkled as they fell on her old friend, the John Deere tractor, patiently waiting to be driven out. She touched it lovingly and was glad she had serviced it before her accident. Elizabeth hooked up the trailer and put her fork, spade, and knee pads into it. She also put in her rake. Struggling, she lifted two twenty-pound bags of topsoil out and put them in, too. She put the key in the starter, turned it, and just like the good friend it had always been, it still needed only two cranks. Its heart began to beat and it started to sing its throaty song. They were in sync again. Elizabeth drove it to the upper garden and began the joyous task of preparing the earth for planting.

The tulips that occupied a portion of the garden were showing their green leaves and she was surprised the rabbits had not eaten them down yet. Their assorted colors would look vibrant against an alyssum backdrop she was about to use as a border here. Elizabeth knelt on the green knee pads and began working the sandy soil as she did every year. She would have to add the topsoil to it and mix it in. She worked slowly and carefully, turning the soil then adding the topsoil to make a proper bed for her flowers. The bags seemed heavy to her unpracticed body as she stood to dump the soil, carefully distributing and working it in. Periodically she had to stand because the kneeling cut the circulation in her legs. She decided to widen the circle that was bordered by rock this year, due to the volume of flowers she had bought, so there were about

30 rocks of varying size to rearrange. About 3:00 p.m. she finished her job. She hadn't even stopped for lunch.

As Elizabeth stood up she felt her old back injury beginning to nag again. She had probably not lifted those rocks or bags the way she should have. She knew her former physical therapist would not have been pleased with her. The old knees also seemed to be protesting their abuse. Well, she never pretended to be twenty, but as she surveyed her work she was extremely pleased with herself and the aches seemed to melt away. She smiled and said, "A job well done, Elizabeth."

Elizabeth picked up her tools, noticing the sun's position; her stomach began to rumble with the thought. She didn't care, though; she was so happy just to be working outside again. However, Elizabeth had learned the hard way to always have something in her pocket to eat in case of another accident. She reached in and got one of those energy bars and the hunger subsided. With everything put back in the tractor, she made her way back to the pole barn. She did not unhitch the trailer and she left the tools, for there would be three more days of this.

Back in the porch, Elizabeth took off her shoes. Then, as she took off the sweatshirt and jeans and dressed in her comfies, she noticed all the dirt under her nails. This was an occupational hazard and one that would occur every time she went to the gardens. After scrubbing them pink she sat down in her favorite chair and contemplated dinner. About an hour later she rose, with a moan, and made herself a hamburger dressed with lettuce, tomatoes and pickles; she accompanied it with a three bean salad and salt and vinegar chips. Later, she had some fresh strawberries and cream with her tea, to finish off her dinner. Finally, an hour later, Elizabeth sat in the spa with the *romantic fire* blazing, looking out at a perfectly clear spring night sky. She always kept some wood nearby just-in-case.

• • •

Elizabeth rose the next morning, "stiff as a board," as her mother used to say. It took her another good soak in the spa to work the kinks out. The arthritis in her knees hurt, too, and she took some pain killers; something she seldom resorted to. Soon she was able to function with little pain. The weather was going to be hot today and she wanted to take advantage of it before the inevitable storm that always follows in this part of the country.

She drove her John Deere, the sound of which pleased the goose very much, and deposited her tools alongside the upper garden. She admired it again for its almost perfect circular shape. Although not usually given to vanity, Elizabeth found when it came to anything mathematically correct, she had to pat herself on the back just a little. Then she went to the house to pick up her trays of flowers that had been resting in the shadiest, coolest, spot she could find. Elizabeth was always so particular with her flowers; any other way of storing them and they would dry out so much faster, she would say.

There were the Forget-Me-Nots and Alyssum which would work nicely in with the Tulips. She also picked up the two varieties of Sage. She intended to plant these six trays before the end of the day. A tall order indeed.

Elizabeth had just gotten the first circle of holes dug when she heard a car coming down the road. She wasn't expecting anyone, and was a little bit annoyed even though she always did enjoy a little company. She just hoped they would see all the work she had to do and not stay long. As the car came down the last little hill by the pole barn she began to smile as wide as the garden she was about to start, and forgot all about her hopes that they would leave soon.

She heard all the commotion and laughter coming from the car and rose to meet it.

"Elizabeth, how in the world are you?"

"A whole lot better, if that is possible, seeing the four of you. Why didn't you phone to tell me you were coming? I didn't know you were back from Arizona. You'll have to tell me all about your adventures this year."

"We wanted to surprise you, and it looks as if we have," said her friend Pat.

"Let me just put these bedding plants in the shade here and my tools in the trailer. You go in and make yourselves at home."

Elizabeth finished and went inside to find her living room full of suitcases.

"Well, let's have something to drink and a bar. I have lemon and chocolate chip," said Elizabeth to her four good friends. "Don't tell me; this was your idea, wasn't it Sarah?"

"No, it was actually the dynamic duo; Joan and Louise. They phoned Pat and me a couple of days ago and said we should come up this weekend if we weren't doing anything. Since none of us had heard much from you since you got out of the hospital, we thought it would be a great idea."

"It certainly was. You will spend the night, won't you?" She laughed looking at the suitcase carpeted floor.

"Secretly, we are prepared to do so," Louise giggled.

"Coffee, tea, something cold? I have Coke, water, or can ice some tea."

After all the drinks and bars were settled on, the four buddies sat down to have a chat.

"You looked quite busy when we pulled up?" asked Joan.

"This was probably the best timing we could have had, right Elizabeth? I mean that if we hadn't come, you would have been on your knees rooting in that dirt all day. Am I right?" Joan backtracked a bit just in case, but sounded quite hopeful and sure of herself anyway.

Everyone laughed at this because they were sure Joan was right. Elizabeth was the workhorse for sure.

"Well, maybe we should have called first, Elizabeth? Perhaps you really are too busy for a visit from us? Maybe it's a bit overwhelming?" Louise asked in her nervously high pitched voice.

"Don't be silly, Louise, Elizabeth is always glad to see us," said Sarah, helping her best friend out.

"Of course it was okay if you didn't phone first, I love surprises," Elizabeth said even though she thought maybe they should have phoned and given her some kind of warning. "And yes, I probably would have been on my knees all day. You saved me!"

"So what have you been doing with yourself?" asked Joan, always wanting to keep the conversation flowing.

"Well, a couple of things. You all know about that goose that lived on my lake this past winter? She has had her goslings, five in all, although, one has been adopted by another family on the lake, I'm sure. I have been documenting their growth and habits through photography each morning, when I can. Then, of course, I have been writing. A couple of days ago Hal took me to get the walking cast off, and yesterday I prepared the garden you saw me working in. It feels so good to be truly out and about again. I feel alive."

"What have you been writing? I bet you are getting ready to publish another book, right?" Pat asked with a twinkle in her eye.

"Yeah, when will we be able to read it?" giggled Louise.

"What is the subject? Or is there just a general theme? Do you have a title yet?" asked Pat.

"Ladies, ladies! One question at a time, please. Much of my work has been centered on the geese this year. The lake and the seasons are a large part of that, too. I'm not even at the publishing stage yet, but have promised my agent I would have it completed by fall. You can read some of what I have done now or you can wait for the book to be finished. I have several copies of different poems that are in it. There is no official title yet, but my working title is Lady of the Lake, although I think that has been used before."

"I love the image that evokes. Is the lady the goose?" asked Sarah.

"Yes and no. The book features not only the goose, but other females too, like a crone."

"Like us!" squeaked Louise. Louise was such a dear, and would give you the shirt off her back, but sometimes her mannerisms wore on Elizabeth.

"Just breath deeply, Elizabeth," she said to herself.

"How about a small hike on the path?" asked Sarah, sensing Elizabeth had said all she wanted to say at this point and she was getting her fill of Louise.

"All right!" the other three enthusiastically chimed in unison.

Elizabeth mouthed a "Thank you" to Sarah.

"Why don't you, Louise and Joan, take the downstairs area for your sleeping and changing quarters. You know you have your own private bathroom down there and it is cooler. Pat, you can sleep upstairs in the loft," said Elizabeth, knowing it was her favorite spot, as she was a very introverted, contemplative person and liked her private time.

"Sarah, you can share my room with me." This would give her a chance to talk to her best friend after everything settled down at night.

They all met downstairs on the porch. Pat and Sarah and Elizabeth were very practical in their dress: jeans, a long sleeve shirt and sensible hiking shoes. Of course, Elizabeth had on her floppy hiking style hat. Louise looked like she was more ready for a stroll in the city park, with her shorts and pink tennis shoes. Elizabeth was at least able to convince her to put on a long sleeve shirt. Louise thought she still had great legs. Joan had a conversational piece on her head, a hat with a raccoon. Pat was very ordinary, as Pat always was. Her baseball cap, sweatshirt, jeans, and sneakers looked like anyone you would meet on any trail, anywhere, in any park.

As they hiked along the paths through the woods, the women gathered flowers. Each had a story to tell. Sarah's story was about her grandmother. Her grandmother loved flowers, but was no romantic. No, she was a naturalist. She believe that the flowers of the earth were put here to be enjoyed and they should be the ones to grace the house. Some of her favorites were Queen Anne's Lace and Brown-Eyed Susan. So Sarah picked flowers for her grandmother, in theory.

They also stopped to take pictures of interesting fallen limbs or plants. Last spring Pat had merged three of the pictures on her computer: one of a log, and one of a nest, and one of the four of them, to form an interesting composition and sent a copy to everyone. They decided it should be an annual crone event and took three different pictures.

The trees were leafing out and the woods had a soft tinted haze to it. As they looked into a stand of poplar it emerged like a Bev Doolittle picture, and you wondered where the animals were. It made for quite a serene scene. They walked by Elizabeth's primitive camp site, one she didn't use anymore, and the grave site of her long time companion of sixteen years, her dog. The site faced a clearing to the lake. Somewhere along the way Louise caught her toe on a root and stumbled, and Joan snagged her raccoon on a limb.

On the way back someone announced their hunger and the five of them decided to have a cookout. Elizabeth said it would be no problem; John had cleaned her fire ring out for her not long ago, while she was still incapable of moving off the deck.

Upon returning, everyone took up a task. The women had brought brats and coleslaw fixings, along with potatoes and eggs, celery, etc. to make salads for the occasion. The pealing and cutting began. As they worked, they sang and listened to music, while Joan played the drum she had brought along. Anyone watching these four friends would have wondered how this bond of friendship had grown.

About six-thirty they were ready to eat. Each woman took a stick, stuck a brat on the end, and cooked it over the fire that Pat and Elizabeth had nursed to the right temperature. The table on the porch had been set for the meal and when finished they enjoyed a cup of coffee by the fire. While they sipped, they had a campfire conversation, with a tall tale or two thrown in. Then, as the sun set and the stars came out, each became absorbed in her own childhood memories around the fire. Before long they were one with the night.

. . .

"Elizabeth, you're up! I didn't even hear you get out of bed."

"I usually get up this time of the day. Want to help me with my camera equipment? I'm going to take it down to the swing."

"Sure."

Sarah and Elizabeth settled themselves onto the swing and it was none too soon. The geese and their family were already searching for their morning grasses. Elizabeth had taken only two photographs lately, since the goslings' changes were slower now. She and Sarah talked quietly.

"You should really give Arizona a chance this fall; enough can't be said about the warmth."

"I might. January, February and March were very harsh this year. My fall got me wondering if maybe this was too much for one woman to do by herself."

"Well, you know how I feel about that." Sarah tenderly hugged her best friend.

"How was Arizona this year? I know you had that consulting you did up here; did it effect your life there?" asked Elizabeth, after a moments acknowledgment of Sarah's concern.

"The plants needed a lot of work when I first arrived. The Myoporum and the Lantana ground covers, were taking over the area. My Bougainvillea died when we went below 30 degrees, three nights in a row. In some places I couldn't even see the landscaping rocks because of the ground covers and then in other places it was bare due to the frost," Sarah said, then seeing concern on Elizabeth's face continued. "One good piece of news this year, the rats were gone," Sarah continued.

"Rats?"

"Yes, I told you about them last year. How they would bring the jumping cholla into the space over the garage, among other items, and build nests. When I got down to Arizona last year I could hear them walking around and scratching overhead at night. It was quite disconcerting."

"Oh, I do remember now."

"Bob, my next door neighbor, put wire screens over the holes where they were coming in and the exterminator put in rat traps. Between the two, my problem was solved. Anyway, as you can see, you would get your work in down there too. I know you would really love the different varieties of plants and trees that one can landscape with. Many of them are of Australian origin or other climates similar to ours. And unless you plan to do some consulting like me, the flowers wouldn't die!" Sarah laughed.

"Aside from work, what else did you do this year?"

"I also went to Second Mesa to see the dances and visit my friends. Pat and I visited the Sichomovi, Walpi, and Hano of the First Mesa; the Mishongnovi, Shungopovi and Sipaulovi of the Second Mesa, as well as the Kykotsmovi of the Third Mesa. Many of the twelve villages held dances this spring; I think I told you that when I wrote. My friend, the katsina carver, and his family live on the Second Mesa. They had invited me to see the dances, since he was dancing in his village there. His village, the Mishongnovi, is of the ram katsinas. The men dressed in costumes with a headdress like a ram and a distinguishing feather attached. The rest of their dress consisted of a skirt, made by the women, ankle bracelets with bells on them, armbands, and sometimes large pieces of silver or silver with turquoise jewelry. The only consistency of dress was the ram headdress. The significance of the many dances were to ask for rain. The Hopi typically only get about 12-1/2 inches a year and they have been in a drought."

"The dance begins at sunrise and lasts until sunset, with breaks for food prepared by the women. They last for three days. The women also provide food for the katsina, husband, boyfriend, or other significant male in their life, to give as gifts by the katsina during the dance. These are fruits and sometimes piki bread, paper thin rolls made from various types of corn; the kachina throw, or hand, to their guests these items during breaks in the dance. There are clowns that give lessons in Hopi ways, especially to their cousins the Pahaana, or non-Indians. The safest place from being humiliated by the clowns is standing on the roofs of the homes facing the plaza. You should never take pictures or applaud during these dances as they are not entertainment but ceremonial."

Elizabeth was smiling and Sarah realized that with her Native American teachings she may know some of what she was telling her. She continued anyway.

"I was given some piki bread and oranges and other fruit."

"Sounds magnificent, and an honor to witness."

"You could come with us next year, if you were to spend the winter down there, you know."

"Yes, I know. Did you make any purchases while on the reservations? Any jewelry or dolls?"

"I bought an overlay styled silver ring at Old Orabi. It is the oldest continuously inhabited village in North America. I must also show you the new doll my friend made for me. It is of the New Traditional style. This style is a return to, but not a copy of, the original Early Traditional styles of the late 1800's. The Early Traditional were meant to hang on the wall, are round and don't have the fine detailed features of the Modern Contemporary ones that I currently have in my collection. They often invoked fear in a young person when they were in the kiva with smoke all around. I am going to begin a collection of them because of their traditional qualities."

"I also bought several pieces of turquoise jewelry, some Hopi, some Navajo, and some Zuni. My favorite piece is a squash blossom necklace. I had always wanted one and was able to afford it this year."

"Good morning you two," Joan and Louise said simultaneously. Pat was close behind, grinning like a cat with something to hide. "What gets you up so early?"

"Just my usual routine," Elizabeth answered.

"We were just talking about Arizona and I was giving Elizabeth a couple of reasons to come down with us next year," Sarah said.

"Maybe even move there," said Pat with that twinkle.

"Is anybody else hungry?" Joan asked. "Let's go to that wonderful, popular, place at the crossroad of B and D this morning. I just love their blueberry pancakes."

"I can't get enough of their biscuits and gravy," Louise commented.

"Make mine potato pancakes," chimed in Sarah and Pat .

Everyone agreed to go and they all piled into the van.

Once there, and having ordered, the conversation turned back to Arizona. Elizabeth's friends were not about to give up waxing eloquently.

"Golfing is marvelous. I found the prettiest course this year in

Queen Valley. It is like a little oasis in the middle of the desert," Louise giggled, forgetting Elizabeth did not golf.

"I live right on a course, you know, and I golf in the Tuesday-Thursday women's league. Notice what a great tan I've got."

"I especially enjoy all the theater there in Phoenix. You could see something different every week if you wanted," chimed in Pat right on cue. She knew, as a former English teacher, how much Elizabeth loved the theater. She also knew, because of the remoteness of where she lived, she hardly ever got to a play.

"Then there is the hiking. Elizabeth, you would really enjoy all the trails within a twenty mile radius from my home. Of course there is also jeeping in the desert. It would be right up your alley. And you know I have a jeep. This year I went to Box Canyon for the first time, and had the time of my life."

Elizabeth didn't take that lightly, coming from Joan. She had hiked some of the best trails in the US; including the Grand Canyon, the Appalachian, and the North Country.

As they told their stories, Elizabeth began to think of all the adventure she was missing out on by staying in one place all year, especially in the winter. Perhaps this would be the year to try a warmer climate for three, maybe even six months. She wondered if she could afford two homes.

Breakfast came and the women ate to their hearts content. They made Elizabeth promise them first read of her new book but didn't push for Arizona any more as they knew they could only go so far before her stubborn streak would set in. Once back, they set about gathering their belongings and in a couple of hours said their goodbyes. As the van disappeared over the hill, Elizabeth's heart sank just a little. It was so enjoyable having her friends around. Maybe Arizona wouldn't be such a bad idea after all.

# Chapter 11

Everyday the geese would take the growing goslings on their walk to eat until their stomachs were full. The grasses would tickle their chests as they followed one of the adult geese taking care of the society that day, and all the goslings would make little high pitched ho-on kinking noises, which were a great irritation to the adults. Then they would stop and wander off and little crunchy munch sounds could be heard. Soon the older geese grew tired and gathered them up in a straight line to continue their walk to the lake. One by one the youngsters splashed in for a swim, always in a straight line. They dipped and played while under the watchful eyes of their daycare providers. The adults could only think of the time when their shift would be over and they would have some sweet farmers' corn. However, when that time came they had to pass their duty on with the admission that a pleasant time had been had by all.

Elizabeth continued to document their habits, rising early as always. She followed their walks and their swims, their dives and their frolics with her camera, so she could later turn the stories that the pictures held into poems. She placed the pictures on a story board daily: the ones she had developed in the dark room she had built in the basement; a room that had once been used for a workbench, which had long since disappeared. The only other occupants of the room were the furnace and the water pump hidden behind bi-fold doors. Today she got out the story board and began to write her poem.

Mustard and Fir: goslings and trees

Haze of the poplar

has settled in,

glowing soft, mash of fir.

Mirrored by other natural beings,

wildlife or tame life, all anew,

soft as mustard fur.


Mother tree, mother goose,

father tree, father gander,

watch coats of fur, seas of fir,

amongst scents of spring.

-Elizabeth Washburn


Geese

Eating till you're full.

Watch the goslings, walk earth's land.

Growing till content.

-Elizabeth Washburn

    The goslings and their families would be pleased, had they known, that the crone told their story with her poems.

• • •

    As the summer residents slowly returned on the weekends, the geese felt more crowded, and a few of these residents felt there were too many of the geese this year; they didn't consider the fact that the geese had been here first. Although usually a yearly occurrence, it felt different this year. Then the returning residents learned of Elizabeth's continual feeding of the one goose all winter and were quite angry. They knew this just added one more family to what was considered an already crowded lake. They, however, did not want to confront

132

Elizabeth because they were convinced she was lonely and needed all the company she could muster. Obviously, they knew nothing of her life when they were not there. They went to the authorities about the geese problem. They didn't know that the rest of the gaggles usually stayed only a day or two before moving on. In fact they knew only what they saw from living in the city: wild geese that had been fed over and over by humans and had become dependent on them so they had changed their patterns and knew nothing of going south or other traditional behaviors. These geese that never left were considered a nuisance in the city parks because they littered the beaches and walking paths, as well as other recreational areas.

The authorities told them they had no options as this was a controlled habitat. The feeding that Elizabeth had done, as far as they knew, was only done in the winter months and only for one goose. The residents argued that, even though it was a controlled habitat, Elizabeth should be reprimanded for feeding the goose. Furthermore, they claimed, in their argument, she should be prohibited from feeding her or the rest of the geese in the future, as one goose will eventually turn into a family. The HSUS tried to apply sanctions even though they knew it was a special case but the DNR, who ultimately managed the region, would not support them.

The authorities finally did agree to talk to her about the issue. They told her that, since geese are an excellent example of a wildlife species whose behavior can be fairly and easily modified by managing the landscape, preventing them from getting extra feed would be the preferred route for her to take. They told her geese would rather swim between water and land but also walk to grazing areas when molting or escorting goslings. If they did became dependent they would not nest where they had to swim, but live close to the food provided. Elizabeth assured them she had stopped the feeding as soon as the ice went out. They also talked to her about the fact that allowing grass and shrubs to grow as little as eighteen inches high, in a 10-foot band around a pond, could act as a deterrent to geese as it impedes their access to grazing on her property, as if she needed a reminder! They were going to encourage the other residents to go this route and would like her to do so, too. It would reduce mowing for her and filter runoff of grass fertilizers and herbicides, dangerous items to the fish and wildlife.

The goose didn't know all this but would have been happy to know that Elizabeth had decided she was going to continue her practices of mowing anyway. The geese had the land first, had a right to feed there, and she did not use any dangerous items that would run off; and, a little goose poop was great fertilizer for her new grass. If her neighbors were so concerned about her feeding a goose they could tell her to her face, although it wouldn't matter. She did agree, however, not to feed any of the gaggles now flying in, so they wouldn't become too tame and be confused over their natural tendency, which was to move on. Of course, this was not a problem because, as she had told the DNR, she only fed the goose when there was ice on the lake.

The authorities accepted her decisions; she was a local so to speak.

# Chapter 12

Rising with the moon's last light, Elizabeth went to take her pictures. Oh, the geese were in great form that morning. They looked like children, learning to dive from a swimming position in the water. Some were definitely more graceful than others. When they came on shore, she snapped three or four more close-ups. Those were the hardest to get.

After having a quick breakfast, Elizabeth went down to her dark room and developed the photos she had taken over the past three days. She went back upstairs and arranged them on the story board, taking off, as she always did, a few of the older ones to make room for the new. She sat on the porch with a cup of coffee and, setting the board on an easel, admired the obvious growth in the goslings. They were almost fledglings now and would soon begin to grow their wings.

Changes

Loss of coat

warmth,

comfort,

safety.


Growth of coat

soft,

functional,

safe.

Keep the secret

secluded,

remote,

safe.

Join the families

swimming,

feeding,

safe.

-Elizabeth Washburn

. . .

Elizabeth dressed in her usual gardening clothes, doing a lot of laundry was not her favorite task, and walked out to the pole barn. She got her transportation and tools and, dropping the tools at the garden, went and picked up her plants. Looking at the time, she realized she only had about two hours before lunch. "Oh well, I'll just have to make the most of it," she said to the flowers. "I've been far too negligent in getting you into your home."

She had drawn up plans for the garden, just as she always did when she used new plants. She began by taking the spade and digging holes in a semicircle around the Tulips, about four inches apart. Into these she planted the tiny Forget-Me-Nots. The next ring, with holes about eight inches apart, held the sweet, white Alyssum. Then another ring of Forget-Me-Nots, another of sweet Alyssum, and so forth, until she had finished those flats.

Elizabeth stood and stretched, looking over the rings of tiny intense blue and white flowers. When they began to spread out and mature, in about three weeks, what a beautiful sight it would be. The multicolored

Tulips would be in full bloom, too, and she would have her first spring garden. She was thinking about this as she returned to the house for some lunch.

She was tired of soup. She was tired of sandwiches. What could she eat? As she stood there in front of the refrigerator she remembered she had some nice left over salad fixings from yesterday. She pulled out red leaf lettuce, escarole, tomatoes, feta cheese, an artichoke, and chick peas. Tossing these together, making a dressing of oil and vinegar with Italian seasonings, and having a glass of freshly made iced tea, she was completely satisfied. Elizabeth cleaned up quickly since the temperature was a balmy 68 degrees today and she wanted to get back to her planting.

One of Elizabeth's favorite flowers was Salvia, or red Sage. Since the upper garden was near the pole barn, she was able to partake of the wonderful sight of these colorful flowers more often than not. It was a most active flower, however, and the hummingbirds loved it. The Salvia would bloom right through fall, once it really started to come into its own in the summer months. Since it was slightly shorter than the deep blue Sage, it would be the first semicircle of flowers on the outside; making the transitional beauty from the multicolored Tulip, to blue Sage, to red Sage, a sight to behold.

Elizabeth dug more holes to put the seedlings of Salvia into. They were placed precisely eight inches apart by using the measurements provided on the handle of the spade. There ended up being six semicircles. She would pinch them throughout the summer to encourage a bushy quality to them.

To complete the garden, Elizabeth planted the rich deep blue mealyup Sage behind the Salvia. It made a wonderful cut flower during the summer through fall months, as it grew from one to three feet in height. Finally, behind the garden area, were the Day Lilies and a large oak tree, that provided the partial shade the flowers needed. To the left was an annual, old fashioned Bearded Iris garden that completed the larger circle of flowers.

At days end, Elizabeth gathered all her tools and put the boxes, that the flats of flowers had come in, into the fire pit to be burned. She finally went in knowing she had spent her day well, as the light-sensitive halogen light on the pole barn shined.

• • •

Checking her list, after an invigorating early morning swim, Elizabeth knew the lake garden would be today's garden of joy. Although she had dearly loved the visit from her friends, she hoped that no one would come down the road to visit today. Lately she'd had more than her share of well-meaning friends. Today she needed to relax and put in the lake garden because it was a good area for reflection on nature's gifts. Elizabeth needed to become one with the circle and the gifts she had been given; this was where it would be found.

The lake garden was small, with sections of natural rocks and logs. She had decided to put the Poppies interspersed with the grasses, so the square area, farthest from the lake and next to the tree line, had been designated for the Snapdragons. She put in some dwarf and some medium tall ones in oranges and pinks. Elizabeth loved to mix colors and this was the garden she would do it in.

To the left of the Snapdragons was a rectangular garden half full of dwarf Morning Glories. These were usually used as a border plant for taller flowers. They would be in full bloom within a couple of weeks making a nice blue color that would complement the many colors of the lake. She left half the rectangle empty because Flowering Cabbage, which had to be planted in late summer, would go in here, too. They had shades of green which would complement the blue of the Morning Glories. Lastly, in fall she would plant some multicolored Mums to fill out the space left by the fading Morning Glories.

To the right, and closest to the lake, Elizabeth would plant her Sunflowers instead of putting them in the butterfly garden. She would have bought the perennial variety this year, but wasn't sure they would survive the harsh winters. She had seen fields of them, though, since the midwest was a large producer of Sunflower seeds, but didn't know if they were planted every year or not. There would be varieties that grew from 6 to 12 inches, the dwarf, and others from 2 to 12 feet in height. She picked the yellow ones, even though they came in reds, oranges, and gold. Yellow, to her, was the color of a Sunflower. One of the most special traits about Sunflowers was that they attracted butterflies and birds. The other was their turning face all day long.

When Elizabeth finished, she placed the rocks and logs back where they had laying, as they twisted and turned to form a path among the different shaped gardens. She walked the path and contemplated the south and summer, her friendships, the natural, and the goose, her totem. She became one, and was at peace as she walk slowly to her cabin, later than usual.

The following day she followed the same schedule. First she put in her major hummingbird and butterfly gardens. She called this her unplanned garden as she drew no plans for it. She knew what she would put into it but she never knew where. This garden perhaps, delighted her most, as it played to her inner child. She could see this garden from her deck when she wrote and it provided inspiration. Elizabeth put two bird baths on either end of it so the birds could take their baths every day and have a drink when they were thirsty. She loved trying to guess which bird species were there, one of the few things she was really not very good at.

There were Petunias of both pastels and bright shades: pink, blue, violet, and reds. Then there was Verbena: intense pinks and purples. These were a very fragrant flower that she would be able to smell, when the wind was right, from the comfort of her deck. She also put in the blue and yellow fragrant Pansy and the bright and pastel shades of Zinnia. These were all planted together, with no defining borders, to give a wildflower appearance to the garden.

Elizabeth finished this garden by putting her different bunny figurines throughout the garden. She even had one sitting on a swing, hanging from ropes in a tree. It had a great big smile on its face.

Finally, working on sheer adrenaline, she put the Impatiens in the wooded, green plant, rock garden outside her porch. It was full of different green plants and trees for shade, like Hostas, Oaks and Birch, with this one exception: a bed of Impatiens at the bottom of the hill where the stone garden path ended.

Satisfied, and happy with the day's work, she was rewarded with an uninterrupted evening of reading. Elizabeth crawled into bed about 9:00 p.m. but at 1:00 a.m. She woke to the sound of an owl. She knew the sound meant death to some Native Americans, her mother's people included. She wondered if a little animal, one of the owl's foods in the chain of life, had met it's end. Soon she slept, for she heard it no more.

# Chapter 13

As the weeks of engaged overindulgence proceeded, the goslings grew to half the size of an adult. If a person could pick one up and weigh it they would find they weighed about seven or eight pounds. They could now be considered fledglings.

The goose's fledglings were still vulnerable but, due to their size, the goose and gander watched them far less than they should have. The youngsters enjoyed themselves in their swims as well as their eating, although their parents would not necessarily know it. Often, as they had since they were goslings, they would disappear under water for a look. From above, the little lights of white underneath their chins disappeared below the surface, looking like fireflies going out. Then, with a bob of their head, almost immediately their little lights came on again. They would then emerge some thirty or forty feet from the brood in this brief period of time. After a while they would have to be gathered in if they did not come on their own.

The goose, like many mothers, had her favorite. The little fledgling was incorrigible. The goose or the gander would always have to round it up when it was time to swim back to land to feed. It looked as though it thought it was a porpoise and was in a constant dive and rise position all day, probably because food was not as important to it. That day was no different.

While the young played, most of the adults fed. Then, of course, since the parents were always hungry, they joined in the feast on Elizabeth's shore. Due to the great care Elizabeth took of her lawn, there were tender morsels breaking through the dead brown grasses of winter kill. After eating and completing their other duties, the families redistributed themselves to their nesting areas. As usual, they slept, in a group, for protection from the nighttime predators. And as the sun set, the clouds started rolling in; by midnight the sky was purely dark.

Every night, at or around midnight, as the world slept, the owl kept vigilant watch over the earth below him; ready to begin his hunt. That was when the small nocturnal animals seemed to be moving about the most, and the most vulnerable young were fast asleep. The former usually had a drink of water, and while drinking they were less than diligent about keeping a watch over what was going on around them. The latter were not under as watchful an eye as during the day.

Since the owl could hear so well, better than any other bird, the slightest sound, even that of lapping water made him look. If an animal was off guard it would swoop down, grab it in its claws and begin its feast. It would tear at the meat with its beak, then swallow its prey whole. The digestive system would assimilate the nutritious portions, but the owl regurgitated the hair, bones, claws, and teeth, in the form of pellets. These pellets, found at the roosting site, could then be examined to determine the diet of a particular owl. The owl of this night liked rodents and small birds. Tonight it had seen the fledglings cuddle up for the night, and had its eye on the small one on the outside of the ring. It could be had with a little skillful swoop.

The fledglings slept well. Their furry little bodies all cuddled together looked like one large dust ball you might find under a sofa that had not seen a vacuum cleaner in years. One little dust ball stretched out, looking like a tangent line, and gave a tiny yawn; the littlest fledgling had moved.

The death cry of the owl came forth, breaking the silence of the night. Swooping down towards the most vulnerable fledgling, it appeared to stop in midair. There was the gander ready for a battle. Flapping its wings, with neck lowered and hissing like a snake, it was ready to take on the owl. As the owl came upon its prey, the gander ran at the owl. As the owl was taking off, trying to avoid what certainly would be a bloody scene, the fledglings awoke. They began to scatter at the noise.

The goose watched the rescue in slow motion from a safe distance, all in a split second. She had not wakened her brood because it had happened too fast. When her brood began to scatter she honked with a reprimand in her voice, so authoritative that even the smallest came to her, wavering on its legs. They were all shaking. The goose gathered them closely into a safe little ball, pushing the smallest toward the center. They began to calm, knowing their mother was close by to protect them, as the owl and the gander fought.

As quickly as it began, the owl moved to another location, thankful he came out of the battle with only a little blood dripping from his wounds. The exhausted fledglings slept peacefully, the circle unbroken this time.

. . .

After the owl had tried to kill her favorite fledgling, the goose began to grow up. She had already lost one of her young and didn't want to be left with only three. She started to protect them better, even though the innocent young grew more and more independent in their ways of thinking every day.

The goose was acting from her heart. She was beginning to prepare for the future. She had the love of a mother for her children. She would have to work at not becoming possessive and controlling. She must teach her young how to train and discipline themselves, so incidents such as last night would not happen again. She must do this with a love that directs, but also lets them make their own mistakes. This would be hard for the goose to do.

She would help them train their sight, to see potential danger, and to return to the protection of the family; she would help them train their hearing so the sounds in the night, meaning possible death, would put them on alert. She would train their sensitivity to changes in the air around them, so the flight of a large winged bird would be felt on their backs.

. . .

Elizabeth had written haiku about this time of youth, the time of the South. It applied to the goose and her fledglings. It was written in 1999.

Tai Chi Chih

Youth, innocent, love.

No one but you and her now.

Learn balanced feelings.

-Elizabeth Washburn

Book 3


The
**Summer**

## **The Fledgling**

I watched the candles

push upward,

in the pines,

towering above the

saplings,

beacons of light.


I recalled

three fuzzes, plus one

fledgling,

that lingered behind,

being rounded up,

and walked

in

line.

-Elizabeth Washburn

# Chapter 1

Although summer had come, according to some northern Wisconsin residents, the calendar and the stars and the crone didn't recognize its true coming until the Summer Solstice. Elizabeth readied herself for this important ceremony to be performed at true noon upon this day. Even if the Sun should have clouds obscuring its view, the rites are expected to invoke the spirit of his rays; if the Sun does shine the spirit will be more glorified and enhanced.

The flower of this ceremony is the Daisy.

The long table was prepared with a gold cloth and candle. A large brass bowl, filled with Earth and glowing embers of charcoal on top, was placed first on the table, before the gold candle. Elsewhere were bunches of buttercups and daisies, small dishes of frankincense and orrisroot, blended well; a vial with a tincture of ambergris; a flask of brandy and a goblet; and a long gold ribbon with tiny gold bells tied to it.

There was also a young tree between five and six feet tall next to the table.

Elizabeth, as custom dictated, dressed in a gold robe with gold ribbons on her wrists, and a necklace and rings of gold. She also wore, upon her head, a bright ring with gold ribbons falling from it. When the clock struck noon she began with the words:

NOW THE SUN STANDS AT THE YEAR'S ZENITH,
AND HIS MIFOLD CREATIONS THRONG
BEFORE HIM: HEAR THEN THEIR
WORDS:

Many chants followed with the use of each item on the table at the appropriate time in the ritual. Finally the tree was taken into the middle of the woods and left there, still adorned. This place would always be considered sacred, and Elizabeth could never revisit the tree there. This was the celebration of the crone.

• • •

The South is the direction of the sun at its highest point on its journey through the seasons. Summer of physical strength, youth and vigor is found here. People prepare, even though there is little or no acknowledgment of it, for the fall and winter of their lives in the season of the south. Symbolically, then, it is a time to prepare for the future. Love, once again, is learned in the South. It is not unconditional love for all that the child had in the East; no, it is the love of one person for another. It is a time of desire to possess and control that person-to have her for ourselves. The lesson to be remembered, though, is that the rose bush underneath holds thorns for anyone that would seize her beauty.

South, on the journey of life, is a place to test the physical body. Its four senses: sight, hearing, taste, and touch, are tested. Many people behave as if they are controlled by these senses, and it is here that a person's discipline is tested; she must gain control of them and not let them control her.

The gift of music is also acquired in the South; the gracefulness of movement, appreciation of the arts, and the powers of discrimination in taste, sight and hearing are gained. One symbol of this, just like the mouse was for the East, is the cougar. The focused concentration learned in the East, becomes a passionate involvement with the world in the South. The traveler learns that idealism makes all things great, possible.

Idealism here, is an emotional response to what is good and what is ugly. The development of emotional capabilities concerning love, loyalty, generosity, compassion and kindness on one hand, and the capacity for anger at violence and injustice on the other are, important lessons of the South, too.

Feelings, like physical capabilities, can be disciplined, too. The most difficult and valuable gift of the South, is to learn and acquire the ability to express feelings openly and freely in ways so others will not be hurt. This will allow a person to become a clear thinker. The Red Willow tree, a great teacher of the South because of its great strength and flexibility, is the symbol of this vital lesson.

Sensed Openly and Lovingly

Butterfly garden,

beauty beholding,

lights up delicate

feelings of love.


All my strength

to not take you

for my own,

lest a bee residing.


Hear the music of the night,

waves not lapping at the shore,

taste the smell,

fill my heart once more.


Butterfly garden,

I have no control,

for you my eyes,

hold dear.

-Elizabeth Washburn

*Denise A White*

## The Traveler Understands You

Into your eyes I look,

pain shows

anger dashed upon you.

I must learn how to control

words coming forth

from deep inside;

to step into your shoes.

I hope never to see

those painful eyes

understanding of mine,

but rather turned to

minds uneven strokes.

-Elizabeth Washburn


## Feelings Expressed Passionately

Gardens grow

beneath my hands,

dirt comes clean

sound your trumpets!

Grace my ears,

wax comes out;

smiling faces

stare at me;

raindrops taste so good.

Keep not the feeling

deep inside,

time stands still.

-Elizabeth Washburn

# Chapter 2

The goose and the gander started losing their feathers about the end of June. They had noticed this one day on Elizabeth's shore. There were a few feathers at first, long ones mostly, but as days ensued the smaller down feathers began to come loose. Instinctively they knew that this was a good thing and, with the great idealism of the young, they began to become very clear in their thinking as to what was happening and what they should do next. It was almost like falling in love all over again, only this time their passion was deeper.

To the crone, as she looked at the feathers on the ground, it could mean only one thing; the geese had begun their molt. This was a time when they would lose all their ability to fly. She documented the activity by taking photographs. She knew not to gather the feathers because birds carried many diseases. In her youth she used to gather them and put them in her hiking hat brim. She had bird feathers from around the world and all over the United States back then. Wisdom Walking had changed all that.

When the crone went to document the growth of the fledglings one morning, there were no geese to be seen. She also searched the area near the other two nesting sites with her binoculars and didn't see any water activity there either. She was unaware of what was happening. Her emotions were high at first, becoming angry at herself, but she calmly returned to the house and began to research geese again. Through her constant years of observation, she was sure she knew all the passages they went through and was totally dismayed. What happens when they molt, besides losing their feathers?

The geese went back to their small island and began to look for a new site to continue their molting. This would be their new place, out of view of the crone. They would not be able to fly and needed to have access to a feeding ground of their own, away from humans as much as possible. Geese become very secretive and need to be secluded during this part of the season.

As they searched the lake they knew there was the larger island, but they were looking for a more grassy-type environment that would be able to sustain a family for the time period they needed to molt and begin the regrowth of their flight feathers. There must be some place on land, yet near the water, that would have all the nutritious grasses they would need. They found it in a cove-like setting. It was set back so the peninsula that jutted out towards the small island protected it from the view of the crone. They could walk to the peninsula and around the cove to find ample food to last during this period of no flights. The only downside of the location was that, as they had noted earlier from their small island nesting site, the grasses were also taller and they would have to keep a more diligent watch out for predators. On the other hand, this was an upside too, since it hid them from view. Pleased with their location, they would remain here for the remainder of the time until they started to grow back their feathers.

The crone was about to find out in her research, that geese were secretive at this period of their lives and she would be lucky to see them for about six weeks or so. Summer would be as it should be, Elizabeth resigned herself.

. . .

Meanwhile, as Elizabeth was coming to terms with the geese leaving her view and being satisfied that her neighbors' "ruffled feathers" (she liked that joke when she had told it to Hal) had been smoothed over, she went about her work. However, talk was still brewing around the lake.

At the beginning of molting season the geese tend to make the seasonal, uninformed residents think they are fighting among themselves for feeding areas. To them, the geese seem to become a particular nuisance at this time; for not only do they leave all their droppings on shore, but now there are feathers mixed in, too. They began to have meetings trying to figure out what action they could take.

"Have the geese been over at your place Phil?"

"Yes, they have. My lawn is a complete mess!"

"Well, the DNR certainly is no help. I asked them again, the other day, what we could do and they said to let the grass grow. Let the grass grow! What in God's name good is that going to do?"

"Jerry, next door, was up here before Memorial Day and I guess he and a couple of other guys had a meeting with the Humane Society. This is the best solution, short of relocation, that they could come up with, I guess," replied Sally.

"Hal told me Elizabeth had been feeding them," Phil said.

"Yes, I heard that, too. Do you think we should talk to her? It can't be good for the problem?"

"I guess Hal suggested that, but no one wanted to take the old gal on. Said she was too fond of the buggers and they were her friends or something."

"Well, something has to be done."

"Actually I don't think there can be, because this is a wildlife preserve. The DNR won't, or can't, even do a roundup; so we are back to square one: grow the grass, or have them overrun us," Phil said sarcastically.

"Or, maybe we will just have to take matters into our own hands."

Meanwhile, the geese were enjoying moving back and forth along the land, in the mornings and evenings when there was the least amount of human activity, until heading for their hiding place.

# Chapter 3

"This morning would be a great morning for a swim. The lake is still clear, the lake is still calm. This young person is in love with her life. The leaves have gone full and the grass glistens like an emerald stone. I could kiss the puffy, yellow-blue, look-like white, clouds overhead if I could just climb that Norwegian pine. The birds sing to each other and I clap out the beat. There goes a robin with a worm in its beak; a butterfly comes and kisses my cheek. Well, maybe that was an exaggeration," Elizabeth sang the made-up tune.

Emerging after her early morning swim, the smile that could be seen on Elizabeth's face, was as great as the sun's rays warming down upon her body. To look at her, most people would probably think she was some eccentric. To many people, though, when a woman reaches a crone's age, like Elizabeth had a few years ago, and has earned the status of a wise woman, they are given leeway to become a bit eccentric. Elizabeth took full advantage of this thinking, and behaved like a twenty-year-old.

She fixed her eggs sunny side up that morning to fit her mood.

Dressing in her t-shirt, with a slogan that read "Crones Nest," her gardening/work jeans, and a pair of old shoes, Elizabeth headed out to the pole barn. She drove the John Deere out and parked it in its special place. Then she walked quickly back to the house. She had forgotten her cap.

Elizabeth had a sprayer in her hand into which she had put an egg, a quarter cup of Tabasco sauce, and old furniture wax. She then filled it with water and went out to the green rock garden next to the porch. Between her and the garden path were her Hostas. The deer had been at them again this spring and if she was to save them at all, she needed to put her secret spray on them. So that's what she did. The furniture

153

wax made the rest of the solution stick to the plants, so when the deer went to eat them all they got was a taste of the other ingredients. It was the best thing she had found yet, and she had tried a lot.

For instance, one of her friends, who raised Hostas to sell, had told her about putting fishing line around the plants. Well, either they had really dumb deer or hers were really smart, being country deer and all, but her hostas didn't make it that year. Of course, all the deer did was jump right over it, or maybe they could just reached them from the outside. She never did catch them at what they were doing, so was never quite sure.

Next on her list was mowing. The grass had gone about two and a half weeks this time due to a lot of rain. This was the first time there had been two good drying days in a row. There was a lot of lawn to mow, more than in previous years because she had opened up her front lawn and seeded it the previous year. There was the lawn around the house, including the path down to the swing, the lawn by the lake that looked like a landing strip, the sides of her part of the road, which was almost a half mile long, and the paths through the woods. Mowing the grass was not a job for a hand mower, in most places, but a job for a large riding mower. Elizabeth's mower mowed a patch a little over three feet wide. Even so, it was obviously a job she couldn't get done in one day.

Elizabeth enjoyed mowing just like she did blowing snow and plowing. Yes, she would get really dirty but that all came in a days work. She started near the backyard of the house. This was where there were the most trees, so she had to use the hand mower to get around them and the fire pit. At noon she quit for lunch.

She had a toasted cheese sandwich and tomato soup to fit her mood of the day.

Once outside again, Elizabeth returned the hand mower to the barn and turned to the John Deere with the mower deck on it. Off she rode, around the house to the front, where the beautiful emerald grass stood. This was her pride and joy and she took extra time to cut it and the path to the swing, so the rows would be nice and straight. On she went to the 'landing strip' using the same methodical ways. Elizabeth carried ice water with her on the tractor and would stop periodically for a drink and to wipe the sweat from her brow. She would also change her mask at these times, as it got quite dirty with grass clippings and dirt. Elizabeth took no chances with her lungs.

Finally, after putting the John Deere mower back, she once again took out the hand mower. She rolled it to the green rock garden and cut the path through it. Then she went down below again and cut the 'island', an area that was built up with trees that the lower turn-around circled.

"Whew! What a day. I hope tomorrow is still nice so I can get the road and woods cut, too. I think I need a nice hot shower before dinner," Elizabeth said to her tractor as she put it away.

The day had been a long one and it was now 7:00 p.m. Elizabeth dumped her work clothes on the porch and stripped to her underwear. As Elizabeth was walking to the bathroom, the phone rang.

"Well, it can ring. They'll leave a message if it is important, right Carl?"

After showering and putting on her soft white robe, she fixed herself an enhanced green salad and a broiled pork chop for dinner.

Elizabeth forgot about the phone call and didn't get the message that night.

# Chapter 4

During the summer, Elizabeth enjoyed sleeping in the loft. It gave her great pleasure to wake up in the morning and look out the trapezoid windows at the trees and the lake. This morning, though, she noticed something she hadn't noticed before; how dirty her windows were. She would have to phone Martin today and set up a time to wash them, and that had to be done before the deck could be stained. The time was coming near for that job to begin, too.

Elizabeth returned from her morning swim, had her breakfast, and went to phone Martin. It was then she noticed the blinking light on her answering machine. "Oh, how could I have forgotten you," she said to the phone. Pushing the button to play, she heard a frantic voice.

"Elizabeth, where is you? Suzy had a miscarriage. Call me as soon as yous can!"

"Oh no!" Elizabeth exclaimed out loud. "Della must think I am an awful friend for not calling back right away."

Quickly she dialed Della's number. She got no answer. What to do now?

Elizabeth tried Gwen's phone; no answer. Well, not unusual. Who else? She tried Carol and even Judy, though she was probably at work. There was no answer at either place. What was going on? Why was no one at home? "Think Elizabeth; think."

"Blair General Hospital, Donna speaking; how may I help you?"

"Can you tell me if you have a patient by the name of Suzy Locke there? She would have probably been brought in last night."

"Let me check. Yes, we do; she's in intensive care. That's all the information I'm allowed to give out at this time."

"Thank you," Elizabeth said as she hung up. Her brow puckered at the words, "Intensive care."

. . .

"Hello Martin this is Elizabeth Washburn... I'm doing fine. Say, I called to see when I can schedule a time to have you do my windows.... Next Thursday would be fine, see you then."

Elizabeth knew there was nothing she could do until she heard from Della so she dressed as usual deciding to work around the house, in her flowers instead of mowing. That way she could hear the phone if it should ring.

She no sooner had set foot outdoors than the telephone began to ring. She ran back up the stairs to get it, not even thinking of her promise to herself after the accident she'd had.

"Elizabeth, I'm so glads to reach you," Della said with relief in her voice. "Suzy losts her baby last night." She started to cry.

"Where are you now, Della?"

"I'm at the hospital with Judy. Carol just left. Oh, Elizabeth it justs breaks my heart."

"Do you want me to come down there? I can leave at any time."

"Woulds you? I just needs a friend to talks with. Judy has gots to go to work and someone has gots to be here when Suzy wakes up."

Wakes up? Was she in a coma? Maybe it was worse than Elizabeth had thought. No, she must just be sleeping. She didn't want to ask for details over the phone since Della was obviously in quite a distressed state of mind. "Will you be okay until I get there?"

"Yes, Judy doesn't haves to leaves for fifteen minutes or so," she said, still sniffling.

"I'll be there as soon as I can. Give me about forty-five minutes."

"Okay. Thanks."

"Good-bye, Della."

As soon as she hung up she started to undress and change clothes. About ten minutes later she was already in her truck and headed down the road.

Elizabeth drove carefully over the curved country roads. Once she got past B and D, the roads became better and she was able to go the speed limit, if not a little faster. She arrived almost an hour after she had hung up.

Elizabeth asked at the front desk where intensive care was and took the elevator to the third floor. As she got off she saw Della sitting there wringing a handkerchief in her hands. Upon seeing Elizabeth she started to cry again and Elizabeth tried to comfort her. Soon the tears were under control and Della began to talk. Not even a tragedy could change that.

"Suzy's husband beens beating her. My sister, Dorothy, had told me a few weeks ago. She couldn't gets here so I said I woulds comes instead. Poor Judy's fit to be tied. Last night it gots to be justs more than Suzy coulds handle and she lefts him after he went back to the bar. Good things she still hads her little car and didn't relies on him. She was driving to Carol's whens this pickup truck cames around the curve on the wrong side of the road and hit the whole left side of her car. She flips over and was hanging out the window when the police and fire department got there. They worked for some time, I guess, gettings her out. They tooks the baby on the ways to the hospital because she had gones into labor. She never even knew what she hads because she beens out ever since." Della had begun to cry again. "They'ves no idea when she will wake up." She could hardly talk now.

Elizabeth took it all in and let Della cry until it seemed like she would choke on her tears. "Here take a drink of water. The main thing is she is okay. They are saying she will come out of it, aren't they?" Elizabeth asked.

"I don't knows, Judy said that. It must be true."

"Well, I will stay with your mother as long as she needs me to, so don't worry about her being alone."

"Thanks; I do need to get back to work, but call me if she wakes up. I'll tell them to get me," Judy said as she left.

• • •

The two women sat there without speaking for quite a period of time. Hospitality came by and asked if either of them wanted a cup of coffee or cookie. Elizabeth took one of each. Della just sat there dazed.

As they sat, Elizabeth couldn't help but wonder how long this abuse had been going on. Did they have her husband in jail or did Suzy actually have to report this. Della obviously knew about it. She had probably been too ashamed to say anything, though. Just then, a doctor came over to Della and said he had some news.

"She is awake, but extremely groggy. We're not sure of the extent of the damage, if any, to her brain at this time. We will have to run further tests now that she is awake. You may see her for a minute or so but don't mention the baby. She doesn't know yet and we don't want to traumatize her any more than she already is, by saying anything."

"Can my friend comes with me?"

"Yes, but for only a minute."

"Suzy, Suzy, cans you hear me? It's your grandma." Della had hold of Elizabeth's hand.

Suzy looked at them but didn't acknowledge what Della had said. The nurse asked them to leave because she needed her rest.

"Elizabeth, dids you sees all them machines? It is justs like in one of them doctor shows on TV."

"Yes, it is. Do you want to phone Judy, or is there someone else I should call?"

"We needs to call Judy. I has her work number. Can you waits here while I gos to the phone and calls her, justs in case?"

"I'll wait."

Suzy looked like she had been beaten pretty badly; bruises around her black eyes and black and blues all over her arms. Where else had he hurt her, she wondered.

"Judy gets off work in an hour. They will lets her gos early today. Wills you stays until she gets here, and then drives me home?"

"Certainly."

From the look in her eyes, the unruly hair, and wrinkled clothes Elizabeth could tell how Della was feeling. She hoped the doctor would give Della a sedative to take tonight. In fact, she would speak to him.

Judy got there a little over an hour later and Elizabeth took Della home. She was quiet all the way. The doctor had given her something to sleep.

"Call me in the morning and I will take you back to the hospital for a visit. Get some sleep."

As the days went by Della's grandaughter got better; there had been no damage to her brain. She would have some very rough times over the loss of the baby, though.

# Chapter 5

Even though the goose didn't want the crone watching her all the time, she watched the crone as much as she could. She would see the crone on the back of the turtle, only this time the turtle was not eating white stuff. Wherever it went, as its belly dragged over the shoots, they became shorter and shorter. She didn't understand this. She knew turtles and they were usually in the water. Now that the white stuff and the hard water were gone, there was no excuse for the turtle not to be in the water. But here the crone was, riding the turtle on land and over the shoots. She knew the turtles sometimes ate geese eggs but had never seen them eat the green shoots like a goose, and in big wide gulps at that. Maybe the turtle was actually helping the crone gather the shoots for her own eating enjoyment. Yes, that must be it because she had never seen the crone eat the shoots with her own beak.

It became a dizzying effect as the turtle took the crone back and forth in the straightest of lines the goose had ever seen. At one point when she could do nothing but stare, the goose thought she had been thrown into an hypnotic state, so she ho-onked. Startled, she rose and went in search of food.

Then there were the days the goose watched and saw the crone fold herself in half and dig with her wings in the plants. All those beautiful, colorful, flowering plants were disturbed by her wings but the crone went on without a care. This never made sense to the goose either, because the crone never ate them. She just placed them in a small nest that she kept by her side. Then the goose thought she saw something on the end of one of the bright plants. Maybe this is how she repaid the turtle. Maybe there were eggs there. The goose couldn't see clearly. The turtle could dig. She was so proud of herself for figuring out how the turtle ate, she had an extra mouth full of tubers that day.

One day, when the goose was watching for the crone and the turtle, she saw the crone by herself on her nest. She became really excited because the crone had not been watching her very much lately. She waited and waited for her eyes to bulge, as she knew this was a sign. Nothing happened. Then she saw why the crone was really there. A sage came up to her nest. They shook each others wings and made noises with their beaks. Then he left. Pretty soon he came back with a platform that was very different than the ones that she had seen used by the other sage. This one was long and it was riddled with holes evenly spaced. As the crone sat on her nest, he took the platform and made it lean against the side of her nest way up where the big, bright, smooth, shiny, reflecting eyes were. Then, into his wings he took a round nest, a long stick, and some white flying pieces and went in-between the legs until he stood on this platform in the sky. He began to flap his wings up and down until the eyes were so bright the goose had to look away. All the while, the crone watched him and not her. This saddened the goose until she remembered that she really didn't want to be found. So she should really be proud of herself that she stayed hidden.

The goose turned away and took a particularly long walk and strutted her stuff. Oh, if Elizabeth could have seen and photographed that, she would have given up watching Martin in a minute. As she walked, the goose mulled over her present situation. The crone was the most interesting thing that was happening at this particular part of the summer, besides her family and her own personal predicament of course. She continued to lose her feathers and wondered if she would have any left and whether they would grow back. As she remembered from last year though, everything came out okay and she was eventually able to fly. The fledglings were having a bit of growth, too, as they began to reach a stage of what might look like a full grown goose. They were beginning to grow their own wings.

# Chapter 6

The days became hotter as summer fast approached July. These were the days that Elizabeth dreaded most. The bugs, and the humidity creeping ever higher, gave her hours of great discomfort. The *no-seeums* bit at her all day and the mosquitoes came out in full force at night, making it virtually impossible to sit on the deck. Her shirt was constantly wet with sweat. A 90 degree day could feel like 105 when the humidity was high enough. Unfortunately, this was also the best time of the summer to stain the deck, as it was usually the driest.

Elizabeth went to the hardware store that morning; she knew what she wanted. She bought opaque stain with just a hint of color, like that of the house. One summer she had painted the deck a solid color and had never been able to quite take it all off. The color was okay, but the deck showed more wear when the paint began to fade in different areas, than it would have if it had no color. Since she did not stain every year, the deck had become less than desirable in color. The opaque stain would not add color and that is what she wanted, just to let the existing or mottled colored shine through.

She took out her faithful tractor and transported her various sanding tools to the front of the house. She strapped on her knee pads, put her coarsest sand paper on her hand sander, and began at the steps in the right hand corner of the deck so she would not be in the direct sun. The deck was as long as the cabin, 28 feet. It was also 6 1/2 feet wide. It would take her at least three days to sand the deck, railings, and steps. This was the part that made her feel her age like no other task on her list, the preparation of the deck for staining.

As the day wore on, Elizabeth poured the water into herself and it ran out with her sweat. She had picked today, due to the rather low temperature of 81 degrees, about average for this time of the year. The humidity was also a low 55%. She would take several breaks, sitting on the Adirondack chair on the deck, looking at the lake, as the bugs rarely flew this high during the day. After lunch, Elizabeth took her second swim of the day and had a nap in her favorite chair on the porch. About 2 p.m. she went back outside and finished the days work about six o'clock. Elizabeth had half the floor done. Tired, and ready for a tall glass of iced tea, she dragged herself into the house to rest. Later she had dinner and fell asleep reading in her chair, not rising until the moon rose over the tallest of trees.

• • •

Every day was a new day for Elizabeth, as she continued to prepare the deck for staining. The following week, after the preparation, the humidity began to climb too high for painting, so she went swimming more and participated in her other favorite outdoor activity, fishing.

Elizabeth was quite the sight when she went fishing. Since the days were pretty buggy now, she covered herself from head to foot, even though it was hot and humid. She had on her old black rain shoes, baggy khaki pants, a worn plaid shirt, and a khaki vest. Of course there was the everlasting, sand-colored, floppy fishing hat to keep her beautiful white hair out of the sun. Pinned to her vest, Elizabeth had lures and hooks for different kinds of fishing. Around her waist she had a belt with a wicker basket hanging off it for her catch, but she never used it anymore preferring a stringer instead. Elizabeth just wore the basket as a reminder of the days when she went fishing with her dad. Pole in hand, she got in her fishing boat and meandered about the lake using only an electric trolling motor.

Elizabeth knew all the right spots for sun fish, crappies, bass, and the bullhead. Daytime was best for the sunfish and crappies. Bullhead fed at any time of the day and she left the late afternoon for the bass.

She took a cooler in her boat and ate her lunch right on the lake. Sometimes she went to the island to sit in the shade of the tall oak trees. Other times, if the sun wasn't too hot, she just anchored her boat and enjoyed the beautiful day. During these times she made sure she had her sleeves rolled up to her elbows to get some sun, so she didn't look completely pale; she had some SPF 15 to slather on, with bug juice in it.

Sometimes, when there was not time to go out in the boat, Elizabeth would fish from her dock. One evening Elizabeth decided to do just that, as the temperature seemed to be breaking. She had seen small bass spawning there earlier in the spring and wondered where the momma and papa bass were. These were her favorite fish because they gave her the most fight. Bass fishing required great patience and Elizabeth could wait with the best of them; soon she was not disappointed. Bam! The bass struck and took her line with it. Every time that bass jumped Elizabeth would reel in a little more line. She fought that fish until she was almost worn out. Finally, Elizabeth brought it to rest on the dock; then she put it on her stringer and set it back in the water to keep the fish fresh. She landed two more sizable ones that evening along with a mosquito or two biting her neck and head. She carried them proudly to the house. About half way up she stopped, put down the fish, continued to the house, and retrieved her tripod and camera. Even Elizabeth was a little vain. She carefully set the camera on the tripod and focused it at a height to take her picture with her fish. She set the timer and moved into position just before it snapped. She took two just to be sure she had a smile on her face. She decided it would go on her Christmas cards that year. There she was in full garb, floppy hat, shirt, vest with lures on it, neck scarf, plaid shirt, and khaki pants. She had one fish on the pole in her left hand and the other ones on a stringer in her right. Her eyes twinkled blue and with her smile and rosy cheeks she was the picture of proud happiness.

She took her photo equipment back and then returned for the fish and her pole. She prepared the fish for a nice fried fish breakfast, what is known as a fisherman's breakfast up North, and relaxed for the evening with the radio and a book.

# Chapter 7

All the while Elizabeth was going about her summer business, the family of geese were going about theirs. Theirs were made up of ritualistic behaviors, too. They searched for the best food, both on shore and off, and watched their parents for hints as to how to be adults. As the parents finished molting, and began to grow back their feathers, the fledglings began acquiring their own wings. The goose observed this daily and wondered if they might leave her before she had her feathers back. She discussed this with the gander and they remembered the stories of how the young had to be taught to fly. They knew the fledglings would not leave soon. This was quite disconcerting to her anyway and she worried constantly, if not about the growth of their wings then about how she would teach them to fly. She knew, though, there was nothing she could do except go about the business of raising them and let nature take its course.

To help take her mind off such matters, the goose continued to watch the crone almost everyday while her family would take a swim. She would see her bent in the middle with legs bent day after day using her extended wings in back and forth motions. She wondered if she was preparing her nest for another brood. If the crone was, though, it would be the biggest nest the goose had ever seen. Every now and then she would take the back of her wing and draw it across her eyes. Then she would stand and go through all these bending motions, and waddle out of sight. After what seemed like forever, long enough for the fledglings to eat, the crone would come back and start all over again. A few days after these ritualistic behaviors, during 'fishing time', the crone grew a stub on the end of one wing and went back and forth all over again on her nest. She didn't bring any vegetation. She didn't pluck any feathers from the top of her head. She just unbent her legs, which the goose never did figure out, dipped the stub in a round hole and made the nest shiny. Once again there was no sage. Then the stub disappeared, the crone sat on the nest and nothing else happened. The crone was a strange creature indeed.

. . .

Everything went along as usual and the goose was happy. Her family was predictable, the crone was predictable and she became content. Then one evening it all changed. The crone got out a nest-like floater and a long stick and floated noisily around the lake and began pulling out fish. Her stick was magical. She would put it in the water and out would come a fish on the end of it twisting and turning and performing all sorts of antics for the crone. Then she would put it on a shiny stick and put it back in the water. So that is what the crone ate when she took them back to her nest, just like the eagles and hawks. She was really a bird that lived on the land just as she had always suspected. Her totem must be a bird. But the goose had found the crone. Then the goose realized she was a bird that lived by the water just like the crone, so she must be the crone's totem. It did not explain the other actions, like riding a turtle or a caterpillar, but she was satisfied to not delve into these areas and continued to think of the crone as a bird; an old, strange, fish-eating bird.

# Chapter 8

Elizabeth had made a bed for her flowering cabbage in late June. Most of the flowers were in bloom then, through early or late fall. Of course the iris and the tulips had come and gone, but the annuals remained. She deadheaded and cut flowers to have on her table, meticulously and with a purpose, so she would not destroy the overall beauty of the gardens. She continued to enjoy their beauty even though she was now working very hard on her deck.

The high humidity had finally broken and Elizabeth, after taking a break from the deck, had heard the distinctive buzzing sound of a wasp. Elizabeth began to sweat and shiver even though it was quite warm. She had been stung, on the foot, at an early age and was highly allergic to their stings, just as she was bees. She must call Gary to come and find the nest and remove it right away.

"Is Gary there?" Elizabeth asked the man on the other end of the line.

"No, he's out on a job."

"This is Elizabeth Washburn and I need to talk to him about the removal of a nest of wasps. Can you tell me where I might reach him?"

"Hi, Elizabeth. Let me give you Gary's cell phone number. Do you have a pencil and paper?"

"Let me get one," thinking everyone had these new fangled phones. "Go ahead."

"It is 298-7626. You can best reach him in about a half an hour; he should be on lunch break then."

"Thanks Dick. Good bye."

. . .

"Gary, this is Elizabeth Washburn. I need your help; an emergency visit. I have a nest of wasps somewhere, and I am highly allergic to them," she said with a slight panic to her voice. She had her inhaler close at hand.

"I can get out there about 4 o'clock."

"Thanks Gary, I'll see you then."

"Oh, I do have a guardian angel after all," she said out loud.

. . .

"Elizabeth, it's Dorothy," the voice said as she picked up the telephone. "Are you coming to the 4th of July picnic? You know it's next Tuesday. All the family will be there; John, Betty, Carol and her husband Paul and the boys and Jackie, Suzy and her husband, Grandpa, Aunt Helen, Marion, Jack, Phil, Hal, Sally, Jerry, Gwen, Judy and her current live in, and Mary and you. We will have the baked beans, hot dogs, hamburgers, and whatever everyone brings to pass. What would you like to bring? I'll count on you for dessert again, okay?"

She took a breath. Like Della, Dorothy could talk without breathing for great periods of time, too, and it was Elizabeth's chance to get a word in edgewise. "I'll be there, of course, Dorothy. I wouldn't miss the chance to have your coleslaw and that homemade lemonade."

"Good, I knew I could count on you. We'll eat around noon, same's usual. Well, got to call everyones else. Good talking to you."

. . .

Gary arrived about 3:45 and took care of the wasp nest while Elizabeth stayed inside.

# Chapter 9

Like clock work, the geese came out of hiding and started joining one another on the land. Troupes of ten and six and fifteen came marching, then sitting, then marching, then stopping and munching until the grass was mowed, and marched toward the woods around the homes, then back. They would start about 5 p.m. and not end until the goose called them to swim to their meeting place around dusk. They looked like a band of disorganized students before a parade, but all moved as a marching band once the lead goose set the pace.

The fledglings were still slowly growing their wings, and their parents were shedding the last of their feathers. They became a nuisance because they could not fly and find other locations and their poop became the worst in years. The lake shore residents became quite overly agitated. Even the tallest of grasses didn't seem to keep them away. The people on the lake swore that this was the worst problem they had ever seen with the geese and they were not about to let it go on. Legally or illegally they would see to it the population was reduced. Secret meetings began being held in homes. Research was done on ways to rid themselves of geese. Even though there were more militant solutions, a peaceful solution was decided upon first.

The decision was to organize a demonstration at the local DNR headquarters. They went door to door with a petition asking the residents to call for a roundup of the geese. They were quite successful and got signatures from all the residents except two; two they never asked. They were not very versed in picketing so their signs were very elementary in nature, but even so they drew media attention, especially since they were calling for a roundup which would take a change in the law.
TAKE THE GEESE HOME!
STOP FEEDING THE GEESE

## ROUND THEM UP
## STOP FOOLING AROUND

They did get a permit and picketed at the end of the week.

The environmentalists from the cities heard about the protest and organized one of their own. It was quite the event in such a small town and most of the residents turned out to watch from the curbs as if it were a TV show. The petition, minus Elizabeth's and Hal's and Gwen's signatures, was handed to the officials. It was a peaceful demonstration.

Meanwhile, the geese continued about their business oblivious to what was going on while the petition got no results. A letter came to the residents explaining why no action could be taken to round the geese up at this point, but it did say that anyone caught feeding them could be fined. The DNR protected them; it did not feed them.

A few nights later, at Phil's home, a secret roundup began to be organized. It was Sally's job to take Elizabeth to town the next day during the time it would happen. Many of them were old enough to remember the procedures first used by wildlife agency programs to relocate Canada goose populations, as they had not all been city born and bred. They also remembered that the same techniques had been used in 1996 in New York, Michigan and then Minnesota, to capture and slaughter the geese.

In the morning, after Elizabeth and Sally left, the roundup began. Some of them took their boats and herded the geese from the water into hidden pens on shore. There they separated them from the fledglings. This forcible separation was extremely traumatic for the birds because of their strong family ties, protectiveness, and devotion to their young. It had been found earlier by the wildlife agencies that without the parental care the fledglings would easily fall victim to predators, if they lasted until fall.

The summer residents were putting them into the back of their trucks, to transport them north to a different lake, when the authorities arrived. Hal had come home from work for lunch and happened to see what was going on. He had fortunately called in time to save the flocks. He never phoned Elizabeth.

# Chapter 10

After another morning swim, Elizabeth cut up the fruit for her dessert. She knew there were always plenty of traditional desserts: cakes, pies, cookies, so her dessert consisted of fruit and a fruit dip. She loved Dorothy's 4th of July picnic.

About 11:40 Elizabeth put her fruit in a container and the dip in another, took out her bicycle and rode down the road. She just didn't do this enough and promised herself that she would ride at least two times a week while the good weather held. Up one hill and down another she rode with the wind in her hair. She got to Dorothy's just about noon, in time to help set up the table. The table was made from two saw horses and a door to accommodate all the food that would be there today.

"Elizabeth, I see you are getting a little exercise today."

"Yes, it was such a beautiful day I just couldn't resist. I need to do this more and it was my way of combining exercise with pleasure. How's Suzy been?"

"She's getting alongs okay, I just wish she would leaves Ken. But don't gets me started."

"Will she be here today?"

"Yes, and so will that no good husband of hers."

"I see Sam, ah Grandpa, is here already. How he still drives that big Lincoln is beyond me." Actually Sam thought of himself as Uncle to everyone and most people referred to him as that, but not Elizabeth; no, she preferred a person's given name.

"He's in the house withs John right now. So is Della."

"Hi, Elizabeth. Thoughts you woulds never gets here!" Della yelled as she descended the back steps. Fortunately, for Elizabeth, Carol and Ted were just pulling up, too.

"Mom!" It was Carol and her family.

"How is my favorite boys and girl? I see yous boys haves grown a foot. Come, gives me a great big kiss. Now Jackie don'ts be shy. Lets sees that pretty dress."

"We got tied up behind some tractor and couldn't go around him because of the curves on D. Do you think he could have pulled over for us? Heavens no, we had to wait 'til he pulled into his farm. Looks like you could use some help. Hi, Elizabeth."

"Carol. It's good to see you."

Grandpa Sam, in his usual fashion, came out of the house and walked right by the ladies without saying a word, and sat down under an oak tree.

Soon, others began to arrive. Hal and Gwen, Judy and her latest from the bars, Suzy and Ken as well as those that had been invited from the lake. Della's Aunt Helen came, with her daughter Mary, about half past the hour. Aunt Helen was 92 and slowing down a little. She was Sam's twin sister.

After filling their plates full of baked beans, potato salad, Jell-O, coleslaw, three bean salad, a hot dog or hamburger, relishes, raw vegetables, and dips and chips, everyone was happily eating and enjoying each others company. Most people had found a table with someone else to enjoy the picnic with. A vigilant eye was also kept on Suzy and Ken.

"Carol, how did the boys do in school this year?" asked Elizabeth. Jackie had just turned five and was not yet in school.

"Bob played baseball and was at the top of his class in math. Barry was in the band; I couldn't be prouder. Do you miss it? Teaching, that is?"

"No," said Elizabeth, with her mouth full of beans. "I left that behind me when I walked out the door and never looked back."

"What a shame. I was hopin' you would be willing to tutor Barry in English this summer. He can't seem to get his verbs and adverbs straight."

"I'm sorry. Can't you find someone from school? An older student perhaps? Did you go to his teacher; she or he? Was there a suggestion?"

"I talked to his teacher and he said that he needs a tutor before next fall. He wasn't very helpful, though, as to how to go about finding one.

But one of my friends suggested an older student, too. I just thought if I could get you to, then I would know I have a good tutor."

Elizabeth stopped a moment and thought. As a crone and an elder, *wisdom walking*, she had a duty to impart knowledge to the young.

"Carol, I would be proud to tutor him. Let's talk about times after we eat."

"Oh, thanks Elizabeth. I don't know what I would do without you."

There was quite a buzz stirring at the next table where Hal, Phil, John, and Linda were sitting. It got louder and louder and everyone else stopped what they were doing to listen.

"Why was yous and those other yahoos trying to round up the geese? Yous knows; it was illegal! I was just glad I saw yous and called the authorities. Can yous imagine how Elizabeth would have felt if I had told her?"

"I don't care about her. What about the rest of us that have to put up with their shit all over our lawns! Jesus, Hal, tell me you were in favor of the geese on your shore."

"The geese don't do any harm. We get to shoot them don't we?" John innocently asked.

"No, you nitwit. We don't!"

"Watch what you're saying there Phil," Uncle uncharacteristically spoke.

"Well, I just don't understand all you *do gooders*. It you were paying the kind of taxes I pay on my place, you wouldn't think twice!"

"You don't need a palace up here," Hal said in a heated voice.

"Listen, Hal, I deserve that place. I work hard for my living and the only escape I have from all the stress is to come up here on the weekends and for my vacation time in the summer. And, if you don't shut the hell up ..." Phil was standing looking down at Hal.

Hal stood too, then became aware of his friends and what he was doing. Phil turned his back on him calling him less than a man, or something like that, and left. Hal wisely let him go. He knew they had already spoiled Dorothy's picnic and Gwen would be hoppin' mad at him as it was.

Conversations began to return to normal, as the rest of the guests tried to find the spirit of the picnic again. Some got up to get some more lemonade or coffee and dessert. They would have something to talk about for days to come, as the *political discussions* had never gotten this far out of hand before.

As Elizabeth peddled home that evening thinking about what she had heard and becoming centered within, as her wisdom took over, she never noticed the humidity had risen.

· · ·

The humidity was unbearable the next day. It was impossible for Elizabeth to dry completely after her swim. She decided to go inside and put on as little as possible, which to Elizabeth meant a t-shirt and baggy shorts. The air was as still as it could be and she decided to sit under the ceiling fan to try and keep cool. She drank some iced tea.

The goose didn't know what humidity was, but felt the unbearable heaviness in the air just the same. She instinctively knew, as Elizabeth did too, that storms were gathering to the west and it would just be a matter of time before they would hit here. It was the only way a hot spell like this could be broken.

While Elizabeth tried to exert as little energy as possible, the goose and her family went about their business. They ate the grasses on the shores and the other items on their vegetarian diet. They dove and played, drank, and came on shore to deposit their slightly digested food about every two hours; and the residents put up with it.

Elizabeth watched the geese and wondered which one was the goose that had spent the winter on her lake. She hoped she had not been too traumatized when the roundup occurred. She couldn't tell them apart any more since they left their nesting site and the other families had joined them for their daily routines. She decided she should do something constructive, since she was going to be uncomfortable anyway, so she got her camera and set it up on the deck to document the geese habits once again.

The goose watched. Soon she saw the crone had those same bulging eyes and sticks and square thing she had occasionally had before. She liked her better when she rode the turtle or rode on a floater and her wing grew a stick, while she pulled fish from the lake, than she did when she watched her. However, the goose had learned not to fear the crone because she always returned to normal and went back to her nest.

As Elizabeth took some pictures of the families she began to think about the fact that she had written very little this summer. When she was done, however, she went down to the dark room to develop her film first. She could use the pictures for her poetry again.

Habits of Two

Morning swimming

graceful glide;

have a mouthful

tasty morsels:

me and you.

Looking out

inquisitive eyes;

like a picture

taking in:

me and you.

-Elizabeth Washburn

• • •

The sky became pea green about 4 p.m. Elizabeth turned on the radio. She caught the tail end of what the weather forecaster was saying, "...and Wyngate County are in a severe thunderstorm watch. This storm has the potential of producing winds in excess of 50 miles per hour. Stay tuned for further updates."

Elizabeth quickly went about the task of fixing herself something to eat. She didn't need to make anything since she had taken some of the cold salads from the picnic. She cut up some fruit she had left. Sitting down next to her radio, Elizabeth ate and listened. As she was finishing her iced tea the weather forecaster was saying the watch had been upgraded to a warning from 6 p.m. to 12 a.m.

Elizabeth quickly cleaned up her dishes and put everything away. Then she calmly went about the task of gathering her flashlight, book light, and book to go to the basement to sit out the storm. There was one more thing she had to do, bring some warmer clothing with her, because even though it would actually feel good right now, the basement with its natural air conditioning would feel cold after the storm had passed. When Elizabeth got to the basement she pulled out the foot of the futon and made it into a reclining bed. Propping herself up with the pillow, she tried to read her book as she listened to the reports coming in on the radio. Then she lost the signal.

She looked out the basement windows. It was about 7:15; she began to feel nervous. The sky was the most sickening, dark pea green she had ever seen. She knew that this kind of a storm was often associated with a tornado. All of sudden the wind came at the house with such a force she could hear the dishes rattle upstairs. Then there was a popping sound and everything turned black. She went to the bathroom, the most protected place in the house.

The popping went on forever, in Elizabeth's mind. Then, all of a sudden, it stopped. She went back to the futon because she knew she could not observe any damage until morning, so she tried to get some sleep. The radio was still silent.

. . .

The goose had never felt anything like this before. Her first instinct was to protect her family. They huddled together in some protective grasses on the island. She was sure a low profile would be best, and tried to wrap her wings around her growing family. The gander did likewise. As the wind blew all around them, and things began to fall toward shore, they huddled lower. The waves whipped at the island and the geese were afraid they might be swept away. They knew they could not ride this out in open water. Then, all of a sudden, it stopped.

# Chapter 11

The telephone lines, as well as the electrical lines, were down all around the lake. Residents were waking, the morning of July 6th, to damage beyond their wildest imagination. No one, though, had as much property damage as Elizabeth.

· · ·

Elizabeth woke to blackness. "My body tells me it should be morning, why isn't it light out?" Elizabeth quietly spoke. She went to the basement window but couldn't see out; the leaves appeared to be plastered to it. She wondered what, if anything, she would find left upstairs. Slowly Elizabeth opened the basement door, fully expecting to see her roof gone, at the very least. To her surprise, everything seemed intact. She walked to the patio windows and then to the back windows, then to the porch. Everywhere she looked there were trees. Most of them had been totally uprooted and were all lying in a straight line, facing in the same direction. They didn't seem to be twisted, like in a tornado, but uprooted just the same. She tried to get out of the house. Only the back steps were partially free.

Elizabeth went back in to see if there was phone service, knowing full well there wouldn't be any. She went back to the porch and contemplated what to do. "Well, first I'll eat." Knowing the power was off she would not want to open the refrigerator any more than she had to, as it could be days before power would be restored. She reached in and took out a bottled water and milk. She kept the water for working around the house in the summer. She could eat cereal and decide what to do.

· · ·

Elizabeth found her steel toed boots, put on her jeans, a long sleeved shirt, and a neck scarf, and took her leather gloves out of her pocket. Putting her pole barn keys into her other pocket she descended the stairs, carefully stepping over some branches in her way. She had to crawl under and over limbs from the trees in her backyard. Fortunately, her first observation that there were trees down everywhere had not been entirely the case, at least not next to the house. Towards the lake it was another story, but that was too much to deal with right now. Elizabeth's main objective was to get herself out and down the road to Hal and Gwen's place. She needed to talk to someone; that's all she knew.

After about fifteen minutes of going through the debris out back, she reached the pole barn. A large tree lay on the roof. There was quite a dent in the steel and Elizabeth was then struck with the fact that this storm may cost her more than her time to clean up. Going inside she found her chain saw and made sure it was full of gas. She fully expected to encounter some downed trees on the road. She didn't get very far when she came across her first.

Normally, Elizabeth would not cut without someone knowing it; cutting alone was ill advised. This was not a normal situation, however, and she started her chain saw. The tree was a scrub oak with about a four or five inch diameter. All she was going to do now, though, was to cut a large enough section, about a foot long, out of it so she could step on by. Elizabeth cut branches and threw off leaves and twigs. This was perhaps the hardest part of cutting a newly fallen tree because they became entangled and, in this case, there was little room to throw or drag them out of the way. It took her a good half hour to get by this one tree. She encountered three more trees of varying sizes before she got to Hal's. He was cutting the few trees that had fallen around his driveway. When he saw her he wasn't surprised.

"I knew yous would be just stubborn enough to cut your own way out. How was it anyway? I've been thinking of coming your way just as soon's I got done here."

"I started about four hours ago. I had about four fairly good sized oak to cut through. It will take me quite a few days to get them all cut up before I can even think about driving out."

Hearing Hal's saw stop, Gwen came outside and called to him, "Hal, why don't you come get some lunch? It's one-thirty."

"Be rights there. Elizabeth is here."

"My suspicions is those popping sounds you heards was that poplar stand yous have down at the end of your piece of yard. They are not a long standing tree. We'll take a look tomorrow right after I takes a look at that pole barn."

"Even though I dread the thought, I hope you're right, Hal; I really hate poplar."

As they came into the house Gwen said, "I can't believe you made it all the way here. We had a lot of branches down and a couple of trees. But here, sit down, you must be exhausted Elizabeth."

"Thank you." Forgetting the rule and not taking off her boots, she sat.

"My radio was so full of static last night I really didn't know what was happening. Then I fell asleep and the batteries went dead."

"We's listened to the radio this morning. We's didn't get a tornado, it was straight line winds. They came at one-hundred miles per hour. Kinda likes a hurricane."

"That must be why all the trees were facing the north this morning. I couldn't imagine what could have done that."

"So what are you going to do now?" Gwen asked as she served them a piece of pie.

"I am going back down and do some more cutting on the way," Elizabeth said wearily.

"I'm going to come down to your place in a couple days and looks the situation over. Then we's can decide what to do."

"Hal, I can't let you take on my problem, too. You have enough to do here first."

"I'm coming bys and that is that."

• • •

Hal came down four days later. He had been able to get through with his tractor as Elizabeth had cut up the trees in the road and stacked them neatly to the sides. She had worked dawn to dusk every day. She had only been able to cut up a couple of trees a day, though. In some cases there wasn't quite as much of the tree lying in the road as in others, so they went a little faster. Her eyes showed how tired she was and her body told her, in no uncertain terms, she was not a spring chicken anymore.

"Well, I sees the first thing we's needs to do is remove that tree from your pole barn. I don't have the equipment here. I'll have to gets it down at the business. I may needs help and I don't knows who might be available. Perhaps John is. I'll go sees him as soon as I'm finished here."

"Have you heard any word about the power, Hal? I'm afraid I will lose all my food soon. I'm also sick of cold beans and cereal. At least I still had a little salad left from the picnic."

"They are supposes to have it on today. I heards them working out on the road. Keeps your fingers crossed. We are in the same boat. Let's take a look at the rest of your property."

As they surveyed the rest of her property it became obvious this was a job for a group of people.

"I can push the trees back a ways but we'll havesta burn as we go. You'll needs a burning permit. We's can go into town tomorrow if yous likes."

"That sounds good to me. I certainly hope John can come down. Perhaps Della and Suzy and her husband can too. I bet Carol and Ted will come over too, if I ask them. Do you think that will be enough people?"

"Yep. I'm going over to sees John now. Yous take care Elizabeth. Yous want to comes for dinner?"

"That would be nice. I'll be there at 6," she said knowing what time they usually ate.

"Sees you then."

. . .

During the ensuing month, Elizabeth's land was cleared of all debris. The 'landing strip' was extended and there was a sky-reaching pile of trees at its end; piles to be burned when the first snow covered the ground. They had been able to burn the small stuff as they went. Neatly stacked close by was a 10' x 4' x 6' foot high log holder of freshly cut logs; it was enough soft wood for a couple of years to come.

Through all of this Elizabeth drew upon the teachings of the South to help see her through.

# Chapter 12

To view the goose and her family after the storm would be to view the miracles of nature. The gale force winds had whipped around them fiercely, but their low profile allowed them to hold their ground and remain in beautiful physical form. When the calm set in, though, their sources of land food had been trampled by the wind. The goose and her family then took their comfort and nourishment from the vast lake grasses that were provided.

There was much to watch as the family dealt with the aftermath of the storm's impact. Elizabeth never saw it, though, because she had more than her hands full. Beaks poked among the sticks to find the vegetation on the shore after having their fill in the water. With an occasional trip up, especially by the feet of the fledglings, and a nose dive forward, they managed to drag up enough vegetation from the bottom of the rubble to satisfy their insatiable hunger.

When she finally took a break from her own needs, the goose looked towards the shore where the crone's nest was. The shore seemed to be all white and green with trees. The grasses they had enjoyed so much were covered over, just like the vegetation here. She so enjoyed the tender morsels of newly grown grass. She cried inside.

This routine had gone on for a couple of days when she heard a sound coming from the crone's shore. There the goose saw the crone on the land with a swarm of bees extending from her wing. They were flying in perfect formation and as they went around and around; but they never seemed to sting her. This was a very strange and disturbingly new occurrence. As the crone came to a white tree it was cut into pieces with the swarming bees. One by one, after the bees stopped, the crone gathered the white wood in her wings and piled it high like she did in the days of the cold. Day after day she did this, never getting stung.

Then she saw the sage riding on the large mouth turtle again. The mouth dragged along the ground and scooped up the green parts of the trees and piled them high. They became all tangled. That day many crones and sages came, although they seemed to move in different ways than the old ones the goose was used to viewing. This happened in the time of the evening sun. They gathered around the sage's piles and set them afire. Then the sage would take his turtle and move more of the trees Elizabeth had cut into piles, and the rest of them would burn them along the way. The goose shivered at the sight. She did not know fire and thought the sun had gone mad and had sent its light back to the crone to punish her for destroying nature. She kept her family on the other side of the lake as everything turned black and the sky filled with smoke, a choking smoke of gray and yellow. The sky at night turned yellow and orange from the controlled fires. They burned every evening for days. Then one morning it was over. The earth lay in ash from where the fires had been and there were only small trails of smoke rising into the morning sun. The goose cried for her lost tree brothers. Then, as she peered through the last of the smoke, she was amazed to see a huge pile of trees, tangled near to the sky, and knew the smoke of the nights before were only appetizers of what destruction was yet to follow.

The goose had observed the crone with much love and admiration. She was the most interesting thing in her life aside from her family. She had watched as the crones and little crones and sages and little sages all walked about removing trees and such from the field of green and white. She had seen the nights of the big sun dance and black tar shoot into the sky. She had seen the morsels return.

The crone had seemed happy, as she always was, when she moved about the land. Her life was not routine, like the gooses own life, but she was content in her own way. As always, the goose appeared to feel the closeness a totem has for its human.

Then one day all the other crones and sages had disappeared. For a while it was only the crone moving about the land, digging and cutting and putting in more flowers with her wings. She was giving back to the land and the sun was burning no more. This had been the day the morsels had started to return. The time of the South was all right.

One beautiful, shimmering, sunny day the crone brought long platform-like things out and began putting all sorts of objects on them. The sight was as beautiful and colorful as the pigment of an evening sunset. The watchful goose, thinking she knew exactly what would happen, waited for her to start doing one of her very strange dances again. She didn't.

The crone disappeared and soon there was pungent smoke coming from somewhere that the goose could not see. As the first drift of air came her way, a whiff of the smoke had a sickening intolerable odor. The goose moved upwind. She now watched the activities. Soon, without warning, all the crones and sages and the little ones appeared again. They all had something in their wings. Some put theirs down on the platforms and some put theirs on the land with a noise. Others had those long sticks on their wings used to pull fish from the lake. After a long while, or what seemed like a long while, they all bent around the platforms and ate, putting things from the platform into their beaks. The goose had never seen anything like this, crones and sages actually putting food into their mouths. She wondered what they were eating. It certainly wasn't anything she had ever seen.

# Chapter 13

If it were not for the gifts of the South, as told by the Medicine Wheel, Elizabeth might not have endured the trials of the aftermath of the storm. She was thankful that the journey never ends and she had been in the South when the storm caused its damage; because it taught her the noble passions of love for her brothers, and of her brothers. It taught her the discipline she needed physically to fulfill her purpose of caring for the earth and how to achieve her goal of restoring her property to the beauty it once had. Not only had she lost at least a hundred trees but also, the new lawn she had put in last fall was quite damaged. It would have to be reseeded. She would need to restore her colorful butterfly garden as well, and it would take much of her creative ability as there had been a tree top laying in it. Since plantings should be in no later than the 10th of June, or so she had been told, any new plants would probably not grow well; but she would try anyway. She felt compassion for Mother Earth and her glories.

Elizabeth had no words to express to her friends and neighbors how she felt about their kindness. She had to rely again on the lessons taught to give her the capacity to express her feelings openly and freely. She didn't want anyone to feel left out or hurt by lack of recognition. She decided to have a party when the cleanup was finished. In the meantime she expressed her feelings in the only other way she knew how and sent them all a card bearing the poem, "Brothers", she had written for them. She also wrote one for her book, to express the gifts that had seen her through.

<u>Brothers</u>

Sensitive of feelings,

you arrived with love,

filling my heart with:

kindness,

generosity,

loyalty,

compassion.

You in the summer

of my

time

set aside

strong feelings

for each other;

helped

me

with my

goal.

-Elizabeth Washburn, dedicated to my neighbors and friends in
Northern Wisconsin

<u>Body Feelings: from Youth to Old Age</u>

I draw upon my youth

with noble passion for my friends.

I draw upon my youth

with determination

to balance development

of my physical body.

I draw upon my youth

with passionate involvement

in the world.


I draw upon my youth

with idealism

that I can reach my goals.


I draw upon my youth

even as my body

says it's old.

-Elizabeth Washburn

. . .

    She invited all her friends and neighbors to the celebration of summer. It was a joyous time and Elizabeth was not going to let what had happened ruin her beautiful place in the scheme of living things. She set her picnic table with many different colors of paper plates and napkins and glasses. She borrowed two tables from Della, one for sitting and one for holding the food. By the time she was finished it looked like a butterfly garden.

People brought dishes to pass and she used her secret recipe to marinate chicken halves to put on the barbeque. She would tell people it contained nothing but oil and vinegar, salt, white pepper, and poultry seasoning; but not the proportions. It blackened well as the flames rose from the oil in the recipe dripping down. It was a sure thing to fix, a winner as they say, and "finger lickin' good".

The day was enjoyed by all who came. There were stories of the storm, some tall as the piles of shrub Elizabeth had burned, told mostly by the adults.

"Marylou and I were sleeping when we heard the first tree fall. I quickly told her to get up and get to the basement. We took cushions from the sofa, water, and a flashlight. We were both shivering and scared. It sounded like living on the streets of the city during a gang war. I knew any minute the roof would come crashing down upon us. Then it happen. Glass started breaking upstairs. I knew it was a tornado. We probably wouldn't make it. So we said our good-byes and prayed," Phil told his story. "Well, it stopped. We were still alive. As morning came I braved my way up the basement stairs. There was glass everywhere. A tree was in the living room. We couldn't get out. We barely got to the bedroom for clothes and shoes. We barely got food. There we sat for five days until the road crew found us. I thought we were going to die."

There were other stories to be told. Some not quite so embellished, some that should have been more so. Thankfully there were horseshoes, compliments of John, and the fishing boat and canoe for those that got tired of listening.

At days end everyone, however, declared there should be an annual storm picnic and Gwen said she would be responsible for one next year.

# Chapter 14

During the land cleanup, Elizabeth had almost forgotten about the July ceremony of the crones. It was performed in late July in recognition of the dark side of the year. How appropriate this seemed, particularly this year. Elizabeth traditionally draped the table with several lengths of rich dark purple and red velvet fabric. She had to buy six candles of reddish-purple color each year on one of her few visits to the cities, usually from a specialty shop. She set these on the table with a wine glass in front of each. This was an important ceremony to invite Sarah, Joan, Pat, Louise and a fifth friend of their choosing to, since it really needed six crones to participate in it. On one side of the table she also placed a large jug of sweet, dark red wine mixed with blackberry brandy and a pinch of cumin seed sprinkled on it. At the other end of the table was a vase for the deepest red roses the ladies would bring from the cities. Finally, wound among all of these things and trailing down from the table, were many different types of vines. A flask of rose, patchouli and lavender oil was placed near the roses and a vial with a tincture of gentian violet was on the table, too.

The crones were clothed in as little as possible with a few long, thin scarves of purple, some rings, earrings and, about the neck, an amulet betokening passion of fertility. These were not all gold as in previous ceremonies.

When the candles were lit the following words were said:
WE WHO HAVE ATTAINED ALL LIFE NOW ASK STILL FURTHER JOY: FOR WHAT IS POWER THAT IT MAY PLEASURE, WHAT IS POWER THAT IT MAY STAND STILL AND REST CONTENT? HAVING LAUGHED AT DEATH, SHOULD WE NOT REJOICE EVEN IN THE REALM WHERE FLESH AND DEATH PREVAIL? TURNED INVINCIBLE,

WE MAY DESCEND UPON OUR CONQUERED LANDS
AND CLAIM OUR SPOIL. WHERE WE HAVE LIVED
BEFORE, FIXED TO EARTH, WE NOW MAY LIVE AGAIN:
THUS, WITH NEW STRENGTH, AS THE LONG VINE
THAT HANGS UPON THE TREE OF LIFE, WE WIND OUR
WISDOM HOME AGAIN AND SEIZE WHAT WE HAVE
WON. NIGHT SHALL BE OUR DRINKING HALL, NO
LONGER HELD BY DEATH AND HIS DULL MINIONS:
CROWD THEM OUT, THOSE JOYLESS HORDES WHO
WILL NOT LAUGH, AND POUR THE WINE OF VICTORY!
AS WE HAVE CONQUERED BLOOD, NOW BLOOD WE
SHALL ENJOY!

At this point the contents of the jug were poured into the glasses and everyone drank and filled their glass again until their face had flushed and their eyes were brilliant. Another set of words was then recited, referring to the tree that had been taken to the woods earlier in the year, and all it and the sun empowered them to be.

The flask of oils was then passed around and poured into their palms. After this the crones anointed one another on their hands, face, and limbs while another chant was recited, referring to the universe and all its natural things.

Upon finishing that chant, each crone kissed the left palm of another. Then they all came forward to the table and received a drop of gentian violet on their left palm which was clenched and opened again until it dried. The final words were then recited six times, and putting out the candles one by one the words, "Put out the candles," were said until it was dark.

Each of the crones then dressed for bed and went to sleep. They rose in the morning and without breakfast, and in complete silence the five went home.

# Chapter 15

Elizabeth thought about throwing out the paper she held in her hand out as she went into the house. Instead she put it in her book, for what purpose she did not know. Maybe it was Sarah's understanding.

• • •

As the days wound themselves into late summer, the fledglings' wings were almost fully developed. The goose and her gander noticed that their feathers had almost completely returned, too. They knew the beauty of teaching their brood another lesson was almost upon them.

The goose also noticed that where the crone had dug around in the spring many flowers had appeared. The green had also come back on shore after the gathering of the crones and sages. The crone continued her routines of sitting on her nest after her morning swims, walking her land, riding her turtle while it ate grass, digging in the flowers, and pulling fish out of the water. All seemed good in the world.

There were still storms, but nothing like the one that had flattened their grasses and blown all of the crone's trees over. The family had learned how to weather anything Mother Nature threw at them. The days seemed to be a little shorter, though, and the goose could begin to feel changes all around her.

Then one day it just happened. She took to the air again. Oh what a glorious feeling it was to feel the air against her face. She flapped her wings effortlessly while proceeding directly to a farmer's field as if controlled by some inner force. Her gander stayed behind, and when she returned he took off in all his bold glory, returning only after he had eaten his fill, too. They both knew tomorrow would be the day.

. . .

After their morning swim and feeding, the goose gathered her brood around her. She told them to watch as she went into the water. Flapping her wings in glory and standing almost completely upright, she took a running start and rose to the sky. She flew a few yards and then, lowering her landing gear, came gracefully down into the lake with a large splash. The gander, then, did likewise. The goose and the gander alternately demonstrated the movements of take off and landing many times. Then the goose took off with the gander close behind her. Upon their final descent, the amazement in the fledglings' eyes was unmistakable. Their mother said it was now their turn.

One by one the fledglings tried to take off. One by one they nose dived back into the water. Elizabeth was capturing all this on film, unbeknownst to the goose. After many tries one of the fledglings got up into the air, flew a few feet, then flipped over and righted itself just inches from the water. At this point, the goose decided that was enough for one day. Lessons were over.

. . .

Everyday the goose and her gander would take their fledglings out on the lake in the afternoon for their daily flight lesson. As comical as it was at first, the goose's patience began to wear thin. The ke-ronking became a little louder at each failed attempt, the tail flipped faster and the legs folded a little tighter. Little did the fledglings know that by September they must learn to fly, for soon thereafter would be their maiden voyage south to unknown lakes.

The problem was also the fault of the goose and the gander. This was their first brood and they had never had to teach flight lessons. There was no flight training school to learn the basics of being a teacher. As the lake became their chalkboard, more exaggerated erasures were observed. The run and extension of wings almost drew their parents off balance and the fledglings laughed silently at the frustration. The goose and gander were sure they had always known how to fly; never once did they consider that they had, only two years ago, been fledglings, too. So they rethought and rethought their methods of teaching and began to take more breaks to eat the tender morsels of just mowed grass on Elizabeth's shore. They finally took off for the farmers' fields to just get a break and cool down while the other family baby-sat their young. Holy snapping turtle, when would this all be over!

When they flew back they could tell the other pair was ready to pull their feathers out so they took over the duty of watching the crèche.

• • •

Early the next morning, after their swim and first feed of the day, the lessons began again. First the goose told them to watch her legs and feet only. Upon take off she looked like a plane taxiing down a runway. As she rose into the blue-green tinted sky, her legs folded back against the rear of her body. She did this over and over, as did the gander. Then they divided the fledglings into two groups. One by one they tried to mimic what their parents had showed them, and each time left the lake their legs were folded a little bit higher.

The second step they showed them was what to do with their tail. Simulating the location of the rudder of the airplane, but the action of its ailerons, they used their tail and moved it up during the motion of rising into the air. They showed them this on land because it was so subtle it was hard to see from the water. The movement was so fast on takeoff, all that could be seen was a little more white of the tail. Taking to the water again they put the two motions together for the fledglings.

Running across the waterway, they rose as their tails flipped upward. They extended their necks and used the arm-like shape of their wings to help them attain a low altitude as their legs folded under their bodies. Then, in full view of the young geese, they turned, coming in for a landing, turning their tails to a downward position and lowering their legs just before touchdown. Finally they taxied a short way on the water before coming to rest in front of their young. Again and again they performed these takeoffs and landings until they were sure the fledglings had seen enough. Good thing, too, as the young geese were hungry and about to abandon the classroom.

Once again the fledglings had a meal, did their duties, and went back to try what they had seen that morning.

• • •

The young geese were beginning to learn to fly by the middle of August, right on schedule. Everyday they could be seen taking off and landing, if not with the grace of their parents, at least feet first. They were more the color of the older geese now. They shone grayer and browner, whiter and blacker in the appropriate areas. What an attractive sight they were, making their short flights over the lake.

One day as Elizabeth was observing their lessons, the goose took off, followed by the fledglings, the yearlings, and finally the gander. They were trying to teach them to fly in the V formation. It was a disaster. Fledgling number two took a flip onto its side and looked as if it was falling out of the sky. The other three didn't quite get the concept of staying in formation and followed suit, probably thinking this was grand play. To the dismay of the goose and gander, the lessons had to end early that day.

Follies

Wind currents grab you.

Sending you tumbling low.

Right yourself and fly.

-Elizabeth Washburn

*Denise A White*

## Letters of Geese Language

Neither 'A' nor 'S'.

Flying out of character.

Return to a 'V'.

-Elizabeth Washburn

# Chapter 16

August days always seemed more easy going to Elizabeth than any of the other summer months. The cicadas and the bullfrogs serenaded ears trained to listen for them. The trees took on a warm hot glow and the breezes always seemed to be washed hot.

Rising early, Elizabeth went for her morning swim that special day and took a little longer to drift by the dock and enjoy the nearly tepid water. The sun had done its job over the summer and turned the lake into a very pleasant swim indeed. She found herself humming "Summertime" as she drifted by.

Stepping onto shore she lay down upon the dock to let the cotton like breezes wash over her tan, leathered body. Once cool as sheets on a cold winter night, the wind now felt like her favorite flannel blanket. As Elizabeth enjoyed the relaxed moment she observed the geese teaching their fledglings to fly. What a wonderful sight it was to see a mother and father teaching their young the lessons of life. She remembered her own mother telling her about her first baby steps.

Back at the cabin Elizabeth had one of the bran muffins she had made the night before, a glass of juice, and a smooth cup of coffee. She lingered while she thought about today and laughed at the thought of having a 'Continental Breakfast' in the woods. Today was the day she would open the secret crawl space built off the loft. It was an annual event and it excited her more than planting flowers in the spring.

This was the time of the year Elizabeth went camping. She never went where the families went; no, hers was a more special type of camping. As she thought about this wonderful event she took down her floppy hat from its peg on the porch and placed it on her bright white hair. Her hat was her faithful friend and companion.

In the drawer, where they always were, were the well worn state and national forest books. Elizabeth turned each page and read it as if she had never read it before. Some of these forests she knew like the many moods of the lake. The only ones she skipped were the ones that didn't have outhouses for she wasn't about to dig a latrine. Even though Elizabeth was as tough as a pioneer, she wasn't twenty anymore. She also had marked the ones with low grounds since she was not fond of waking up in the middle of a mud field.

As she read through the pages she noted which forests had the best steams and small lakes. She would take a book, another companion and also use much of her time writing the ending of her book, "Lady of The Lake." She would make sure, though, that the wildlife she wrote about consisted of those birds found on her lake, as well as deer and bear, and not those from where she was camping. She stopped to reflect on the year she had not strung her food high enough and far enough from the tree at night and a bear had gotten it. She was just lucky she had not had a midnight snack in her tent or become a midnight snack. She reflected as well on the other years: the year of the trout, the year of the turtles, and the year of the fire, that she barely escaped.

Narrowing her choices, she finally picked an area of the Chequamegon-Nicolet National Forest. It was a place she knew so well, yet not at all. Many of her Native American friends were of the Lac Du Flambeau Indian Tribe and had shown her this part of the forest. This year she would camp near Anvil Lake National Forest Campground west of Eagle River. Set in northern Wisconsin, it was a good day's drive from her home.

Elizabeth turned off the ringer on her phone and climbed the stairs to the loft. With great anticipation she opened the door to the crawl space. Inside she found an array of camping gear that had been put neatly away last year. She took out her backpack with its internal frame and began her work opening every zipper and pocket on the pack. It always amazed her how much room there was in a suitcase you carried on your back. She never took more than would fit into the space as she would have to pack everything into her site, down a long trail. She found her nested cups, her compacted utensils, and her collapsible washing pan. There was the 2"x 3" head lamp for reading her book and making trips to the outhouse in the night. She also found the space saving towel and freeze dried food she had purchased on sale at the end of last season. Then there was the backpacking stove, her backpacking tent, and the new aluminum chair (the other had collapsed last year and she'd had to sit on a log at her campfire for five days). Finally, she found, neatly draped, her Thermal Rest mattress and her largest item, the down sleeping bag. As she gave one last look around, she discovered she had missed the wind proof, water proof matches, compass, bug repellant and her rain poncho. She also had to get her boots, fishing pole and writing materials that had been left downstairs, ready to go.

After gathering all her equipment she began to daydream about fishing for trout, hiking the trails, reading her book, and writing her poems. So pleasant were her thoughts, she had almost lost track of time when her stomach reminded her it was time for dinner.

Tomorrow she would begin her packing and unpacking. Three times she would do this as she also had her two pair of panties, one to wear and one to wash every day, two pairs of hiking socks, her camping pants, shorts, shirts and wool shirt to fit in. She also had to make room for her moccasins to be used as camp shoes; her hiking boots were strictly for the times she was away from camp. She had learned from experience that everything grew in a week if you didn't practice first.

Elizabeth went down the stairs happy, hungry, and content at the day's accomplishments.

. . .

While the geese gave flight lessons, Elizabeth finished her preparations for camping. She had unpacked her pack and packed it the requisite three times and everything fit perfectly. As she finished packing, tying her sleeping bag and tent to the top of the backpack and strapping her fishing pole and chairs to its sides, she thought of the nights she would spend away from all her chores and her serene lake. Into her vest pocket she put her license, lest she be fined while fishing. The last thing she put in - she had almost overlooked - was her camping diary. She always kept track of each day's events on her trip, especially any unusual encounters. She knew the trip was good for her but also knew that after a week she would be itching to return.

Elizabeth slept well that night, serenaded by the loons. She awoke at 5 a.m. and had a hardy breakfast before embarking on her trip. Into her truck she placed her pack and took some extra granola bars in the cab. Except for a bathroom break she would not stop until she reached her destination. It was imperative she set up camp before nightfall, which comes earlier in the dark of the forest.

Crossing into the Chequamegon-Nicolet Forest area, her heart began to beat a little faster. The closer she got to her destination, the more the smile on her face widened. She began to sing campfire songs to herself and soon arrived. It took about a half hour to find a site that had not been taken, within hiking distance of a small body of water.

Elizabeth set up her tent about six feet from the fire pit. The ground was soft, due to all the rain they had had here this summer, which made pitching her tent easy. She then gathered dead fall wood for the evening fire and hiked to the lake to see if she could catch a few fish for her evening meal. The light was beginning to fade as she got back to her home in the woods. Building a fire first, then skinning her bass, she sat down to eat about 5 o'clock, and finished as the last light faded from the sky.

Upon finishing her meal and cleaning up, into her diary Elizabeth wrote, "Today was most satisfying. I arrived at camp in time to do a little fishing and have my meal in relative daylight. As I sit by the fire I think of the many times I have not had the luxury of having fresh fish at night. I feel so privileged, at my age, to be able to still enjoy the comforts of the woods on a summers' eve."

About eight o'clock she went to the outhouse, came back to camp, brushed her teeth with water she had gathered in her pan from the brook that fed the pond, climbed into her flannel pajamas, and took her book into the tent to read a bit, before going to sleep.

• • •

Elizabeth rose and put on her wool shirt, as she suspected she would have to do every morning, before she sat down to write. She had already started the fire to keep warm, before the sun had a chance to penetrate the forest canopy, while she was still in her pajamas, then crawled back into her bag to warm up before getting dressed. When she was in the woods Elizabeth always seemed to write before she ate, and this morning was no exception. Later she would have her freeze dried pancakes and coffee.

Dew

Drips run down as you emerge,

from your morning swim

through nights air so thick,

matching droplets on towering

pine.  You shake just at the

moment wind moves the needles,

sending bubbles of rain tumbling

to the ground.

-Elizabeth Washburn


Life's Elemental Purpose

Gathering,

simple,

functions,

life's choices,

bearing gifts.

Given ancestors:

fire,

water,

air,

earth,

living for cause.

Given circle:

lives entangle,

gifts.

Given purpose:

sacred

graces

all.

-Elizabeth Washburn

Elizabeth took the rest of her gear out of her backpack to lighten it. She then replaced the mix of MM's, raisins, and nuts, granola bars, a bottle of water, her knife, her rain poncho, matches, headlight, the extra pair of socks, and bug repellent. Changing out of her moccasins and into her hiking boots, she looked like an authentic woodswoman. She put her compass into her vest pocket, after taking a reading and locating where she was on the topographical map provided at the entrance, which she had also put into her pocket. She decided to hike a trail that would take her to another lake about six miles into the woods.

Elizabeth reached her destination about one o'clock and sat on a rock next to the lake. Taking the pack off her back felt like she had instantly shed about ten pounds. She took off her boots and socks and let the minnows swimming nearby nibble and tickle her feet. She also removed her wool shirt and felt the warmth of the sun lick her skin. Elizabeth took out her trail mix and began to eat handfuls of it. This would give her the energy she needed to make the hike back to camp. She reflected on how easy the trail had been to follow. Well, after all, it did take a lot to challenge her. The mosquitoes found her arms quickly and she had to apply her repellent. She also reapplied it to her neck and hands to be on the safe side. Taking out her map Elizabeth decided to take an almost parallel trail on her way back. It looked like the terrain might be a little harder to traverse, and she felt like working her body.

Returning her boots and socks to her feet and her shirt to the pack along with everything else, but the map and compass, Elizabeth set out for camp about two, giving herself plenty of time to get back.

Several times Elizabeth had to stop, the underbrush was so thick, and check her map and compass. This trail was virtually nonexistent, not at all like the one she had taken on the way up to the lake. About four o'clock she began to become a bit concerned as the sunlight was beginning to disappear. Then, all of a sudden, she saw the camp.

•  •  •

Having overdone it the first day, even for a pioneer like herself, the hike dictated the pace of the rest of the week. She took short, two mile hikes each day, did some fishing, but not always with the same success of the first night, a lot of writing and some reading at her campsite. Upon the seventh day, as she was packing, Elizabeth surprised herself when a couple of tears rolled down her face.

# Chapter 17

Elizabeth went outside, in the middle of August after the sun had set, with a cup of coffee, her camera and tripod, special lens, and a light blanket. She set up her equipment, pointed toward Perseus and waited. Throughout the night she watched and took black and white pictures of the spectacular meteor showers. They were coming at nearly fifteen a minute at some points. Her only breaks were for additional cups of coffee and to relieve herself.

The next evening, instead of her camera, she proceeded to cover the long table at sunset with a cloth of pale orange silk. Upon it she sat five orange candles with a rusted container of twigs containing faded leaves, stinging nettle, and Artemisia. On the other side was a cup of cider vinegar mixed with bitter vermouth. Finally, in the center, she sat pottery full of roadside dust and a long, coiled, silver ribbon.

Elizabeth had dressed in a rust-red pants suit from the 70's with a silver chain around her neck. She lit the candles and said,

NOW SUN TARNISHES, HIS RUDDY FIRE COOLS, NOW HAZE AND DARKNESS VEIL HIS RUSTED GOLD: SOON STARS WILL TOPPLE DOWN THE HEAVY SKY, WILL HEADLONG FALL, FLAIL THEIR RAYS LIKE GIDDY FOOLS, FAINTING, DRUNKEN FROM ALL SUMMER'S DRAUGHTS, AND FALL WITH A MUTED CHIME, AS OF SAD BELLS THAT FAIL: NOR ARE THESE STARS, BUT ONLY MOTES OF STARS CAST OUT FROM HEAVEN, WASTED ON THE AIR, TRAILING THEMSELVES TO MERE MISTS BEFORE THEY DIE: SO BLEEDS THE SUN, IN SPARKS OF WITHERED DUST, NOT EVEN SPENDING BLOOD, BUT DRAWN TO DROUGHT: A VOID WHOSE

DEEPEST WOUND MAY YIELD NO MORE THAN DRY CHAFF BLOWN ACROSS A BLIGHTED FIELD.

She uncoiled the ribbon and held it in both hands and said words that spoke of the love of the sun and its cooling, now that summer was waning. The ribbon was once again wound, this time around Elizabeth's hands and wrists, while she said words that referred to the sun's cooling effect.

Then again the ribbon was used, this time knotted around her left wrist while her words continued to speak of the changing of the stars positions in the sky. The contents of the cup were tasted and the ribbon untied as the ceremony continued in this vein.

The final two acts were to shower the ribbon, which had now been untied and placed on the table, with dust to signify the slow death that is coming during the season, and then leaves and such were pressed between her hands while Elizabeth bowed her head and blew out the candles.

• • •

The ceremony Elizabeth, the crone, had performed may have talked of cooling days, but these were the 'dog days of summer.' The geese seemed to be stuck in time and, except for the chores she absolutely had to do, Elizabeth sat in her chair most of the day.

The air hung heavy all around and the papers on her lap curled at the edges. She looked at her work through her teacher's eyes, not accepting that its quality was worthy of publishing. She struggled not to rip up the damp pages scattered about the floor. The first draft looked like a train wreck and she wondered if she could ever write another word.

The fan blew hot air on her scantly clad body. She put the glass of iced tea up to her face and tried to cool down. The phone rang. Dragging her damp body up from her chair, she reluctantly answered it.

"Elizabeth, hi," the recognizable voice came across the airways with a smile on the caller's face.

"Hi. Where are you?"

"Close." Somehow Elizabeth expected this answer.

"What are you doing so far from home on such a beastly day?"

"I thought my air-conditioned car and a visit to my best friend would be a nice summer diversion. I'm about 20 minutes away and thought you might like to head on up to the North Shore for a late lunch or early dinner?" Sarah asked knowing Elizabeth couldn't resist. "Anyway if you are up to it, get yourself dressed and be ready for a little adventure."

"You just made my day. I'll be ready."

Elizabeth showered and dressed in her yellow walking shorts and matching striped shirt. She combed her hair. She heard Sarah's car turn into the drive just as she was putting on her pair of Tevas.

Sarah was greeted at the door with a huge smile and hug from Elizabeth. Both women, looking as fresh as a spring day, climbed into the car and were off on their adventure.

"So, what have you been up to lately?" Elizabeth asked.

"Well, I've been going to a lot of outdoor concerts at the History Museum, with the ladies, and doing my usual biking."

"Who's been there?"

"Bluedog, New Riverside Ramblers, and Five Mile Chase."

"You certainly enjoy varied performances."

"The Minnesota State Fair is coming up. Would you like to come down on Senior Day? We can go to the concerts at the different band shells as well as enjoy the exhibit halls and the Pronto Pups."

"You know I wouldn't miss it for the world."

"So, Elizabeth, how's your book coming?"

"It's just awful. I can't, for the life of me, understand why I wrote some of that stuff."

Sarah just laughed, knowing how good Elizabeth was and how she always went into a self-hate mode toward the end of a project.

As they drove past the trees of summer they talked and enjoyed each others company.

It was late afternoon before they arrived in Superior. They crossed over the bridge, across the lake and found themselves at Grandma's Restaurant. They served the best hamburgers in the world, according to Elizabeth, and she never even looked at the menu while Sarah decided on something new. As they ate they plotted out the rest of their day.

"Let's walk the boardwalk. Then let's cruise the tourist shops for some memorabilia," Elizabeth said and Sarah agreed.

The two friends strolled while the bicyclists and the, mostly under forty, inline skaters enjoyed the turns and hills of a paved path on the long boardwalk. When they returned they each went into different stores to buy that one piece that reminded them most about the day.

They both smiled when they exchanged the gifts, as was their tradition. Elizabeth had bought some honey essence soap that reminded her of the sweetness of the day and Sarah had gotten a miniature sailboat in a bottle that reminded her of the fresh breeze.

Not arriving back at the cabin until well after 9 p.m., the friends drank a cup of white tea and went to bed; each was thinking of the day as they slept with their gift under their pillows. To Elizabeth, the gift was another symbol gathered on her journey this year.

# Chapter 18

The dominant totem, of which the goose was part of the clan, was the black bear. As the goose met the challenges of teaching her young to fly, she reflected on the teachings of the black bear. It taught her that the greatest strength came from within. When storms from the sky come, as they did last night, she now knew how to draw upon that strength. So during her loafing period of those oppressive August days, she reflected on the teachings of this symbol of the West, the direction into which the wheel now moved as the winds and life began to change.

The days of heat and high humidity were always followed by crashes of thunder and lightning that often came from the West. They, symbolically, were a source of great power. This power would help her In training her young. Her power was renewed every time there were humidity-breaking storms.

Just like the crone, she too became despondent with her teachings at times. Watching the fledglings make error after error, day after day, was enough to make even the most patient goose want to quit. She would remember, however, where her roots were and try again. These teachings, even though they were her first as an adult bird, were learned with the fortitude of a scholar.

Today the parents would try to take their young on their first real flight. Today they would go as a family to a farmer's field. They had not tried a landing on land before so it would also be a challenge of great proportions. Today they would bring the first sign to the end of summer, even though they did not know this.

After their morning swim and review of take off, landings, and flying in formation (this was still a confusing concept as the young had always followed in a straight line before), the flock flew into the sun.

The geese actually looked like they were a V to the casual observer on land who looked up when they heard their honking overhead. There were even those who swore winter was coming early, probably by October, due to these observations.

The gander landed first with his feet stretched forward and his neck extended down. It was the first fledgling's turn. It mimicked the movements of its father but tried to run just like he had been taught to do in the water. He went forward and his head skimmed the ground. The next two did the same thing. The last one, having observed its brother and sisters' mistakes, put down more smoothly, like a plane pulling up short. The goose was last. As least everyone was intact.

The geese, sharing the area with many other birds, ate their fill. The fledglings were particularly pleased with their landing and celebrated with more food than they normally would eat. After a days worth of seed they took off, much better than they landed, flew back to the lake, preened and drank and had a celebration. They all knew this had been a very special day indeed. Something new was on the horizon.

# Chapter 19

Elizabeth felt exhilarated by yesterdays outing. She took time to be alone and meditate the following morning remembering the teachings of the black bear and turtle when she journeyed to the West. After Sarah rose and they had a light breakfast, Sarah left; Elizabeth felt ready for the challenge of the assembly of her book. She knew she was still in the writing and rewriting stage and used all her inner strength to attack the days work.

Maybe it was the power the storms had brought last night, maybe it was the dry cool air that morning, or maybe it was her harmonious nature with the great universal teachings, but she felt a great strength from within and was able to shut out the clamor of the world. She knew that turtle also had a part in the learning she had experienced here. It had granted her the gift of perseverance by learning his ways. She supposed this was why she had felt the need to meditate this morning and experience deep personal reflection.

Finding the Unknown

I go within,

experiencing

my dreams,

my strengths,

my humility,

my reflections.

I am alone with myself.

Fasting within,

drawing

my powers,

my spirituality,

I have vision.

-Elizabeth Washburn

Elizabeth's will was tested that day. Words danced across the pages as if her fingers had choreographed them. Lunchtime and dinner were just arbitrary times on the clock that she never checked. From time to time the commitment to what she valued most was almost excessive, but Elizabeth never saw it. She respected others' struggles and she respected her own, so anything was possible that day; and just before the sun broke the horizon she put her pen down. She had completed the last poem of the summer.

Struggle

Challenged by days

exercises,

fresh breeze over

honey soap

washes me with

powers,

strengths,

stirring my

*Denise A White*

rise to grasp

dreams,

ceremony,

humility,

acknowledged in

prayer.

-Elizabeth Washburn

Book 4

**The
Fall**

## <u>Gathering Geese</u>

Learning flight

we gather together,

taking care of each other

in community.


Feeling part

of the whole

we dance our dreams,

as reality awaits

in our reunions.

-Elizabeth Washburn

# Chapter 1

To Elizabeth, the letters on the page were brought out by her child and gave her life.

. . .

    The lake seemed alive during late September. The ducks and their families lazily swam around the lake, teeming with the activity of geese business once more. The adult families were still having a terrible time educating their young. The yearlings were digressing. The adults were puzzled, since the yearlings had wings and they could fly. They had even gone with the juveniles sometimes or had taken several flights on their own to the fields close by. But then the yearlings would get in the way of the lessons they were trying to give to their young, and even bothered other families. The juveniles were becoming a bit more interested in other activities so were not quite the nuisance they had once been, still having their moments, though, when they, too, vied for attention. As the days went on it became clear to the adults that the family might not even be ready to fly South. They might have to be part of a later migration. They were getting headaches. It was hard having young and one and two year olds all at once. Their youngest were anxious to learn the techniques of flight and didn't quite understand why their brothers and sisters were always making trouble. They had their wing feathers now and could fly. If just given the chance to practice more and get better, they would be ready for the migration on time. It was as if the one and two year olds didn't want to give up any attention, so they would make up things to fight about, and all their parents' time would be spent with them and not teaching all the techniques of migration.

    The older adults on the lake were not the only ones bothered by the antics. The goose and gander had their problems too, only theirs were more acute since this was the first time they had ever taught the techniques of migration and flight. Why the goose herself didn't even choose to migrate last year so she had no idea of what they were in for. The other family's problems became theirs, because the yearlings would situate themselves right between both families and wait for attention. This hindered their teaching progress because they were trying to learn from the adults through observation. No wonder the lake seemed alive; it was.

As September became October and the teaching nightmares a thing of the past, more flocks of geese began showing up on the lake on their migration South. For some it was a reunion, for some it was in search of a new gaggle to join. These were younger geese that had lost their nests or goslings to other misfortunes and left early, or older adults that had had their young at an earlier time in the spring. With more families around, the goose and gander found it was hard to keep track of their own. Some days the goose and gander gave up in utter frustration and just swam and frolicked in the water themselves. Most days though, they learned as much as they could about the migration and taught it to their young. They felt they would be ready by the time the ice of the lake began to come.

One day, though, while swimming and preening, the goose had a strange feeling wash over her. She looked toward the shore and saw the crone and as the clouds passed over the goose, she felt she might make a different decision altogether.

· · ·

The gathering geese reminded Elizabeth that summer was about to change to fall. That meant the ceremony of the Autumnal Equinox, had to be prepared. She rued this time of the year, in spite of the magnificent colors, for the fact that the life around her would become dormant once more. The crones looked upon this period of time as the Sun's rays bending toward the lengthening days of darkness. This was one ceremony she didn't want to perform because it symbolically represented a period of death.

Elizabeth phoned her friends. She knew this was a time of preparation for them too, a time of leaving behind the beauties of a summer filled with the lingering warmth of the green landscape, a time to leave for the desert landscape. She also knew that this year she had to make a decision she had been putting off for the many years of her retirement. She looked at the geese and wondered what her goose would decide.

Elizabeth went and gathered the withered thistle, balm of rue, incense, old wooden box, and the clock and glass she always used in the ceremony. On the Autumnal Equinox her friends arrived, settled in, and the preparations began.

Dressed in their oldest, worn and almost threadbare clothing, with old gray veils to cover their hair, the crones prepared the table for the ceremony. On the table they placed rags, that once had been clothing. At one end of the tables Elizabeth placed a balm of rue and thickly smoking incense at the other. In the center was the clock whose ticking signified the passage of time. There were the dried stalks of old, withered thistles on the table, and the old, wooden box with the glass of water inside it. The box was placed in front of the clock. At the exact moment the Sun set, they all stood in front of the table and began their chant: NOW THE SUN IS OVERWHELMED, AND WE ARE LEFT ALONE TO DIE; WITH ALL THE FADED TREES, THE WASTED FLOWERS, DO WE ALSO FADE AND WASTE... AND ALL OUR SENSES, OUR DELIGHTS, TURNED PALE AND LEACHED OF TASTE, PALED TO A SCENTLESS DROUGHT THAT RUSTS THE HEART TO A MERE FOOLISH TICKING CLOCK.

At this point a moment of silence was observed as they became aware of the tick of the clock. Then these words were spoken three times in rhythm with its ticking:

THE BRAIN
MUST BREAK
THE BONE
MUST CRACK
THE BLOOD
MUST CLOT
THE HEART
MUST STOP
THE FLESH
MUST ROT.

All of the crones then anointed their hands and faces with the balm of rue and knelt upon the floor with bowed heads and recited the third set of words; after which each person drank a little of the water and the fourth part was recited.

The jar of thistles was then held up and they said:
EVEN THE KING
GROWS OLD AND WHITE
WHEN ROYAL NOON
HAS TURNED TO NIGHT:
YET BETTER THE PEACE
OF THISTLEDOWN
THAN POWER UNDER
A THORNY CROWN.

The thistles were crushed into the wooden box with these words:
LET HIM SLEEP
HIS SLEEP OF GRAY
WHERE GOLD AND PURPLE
FALL AWAY,
AND LET US LIE
BESIDE HIM HERE,
PAST PAIN OR JOY,
DESIRE OR FEAR.

Pat then covered the box with her veil and before the altar asked a series of three questions, answered by Sarah in turn. When this concluded, everyone went to their rooms. Later Elizabeth took the thistles to her fireplace and burned them.

After all the things were put away and the friends had dressed again, they talked of winter plans. Elizabeth was asked many times if she would join them in Arizona this year and all she would say is, "It depends on a goose."

· · ·

Elizabeth felt that she he no time for her inner life and had felt signs of a spiritual emptiness. Perhaps it was the ceremonies, maybe the migrating geese, but she expected it was the lack of attention she had been paying to her ancestors. She was like a gosling before it grew its wings. Her lack of meditation was probably responsible for her feelings. One part of her had been lost, lost within her physical, emotional and mental state. She knew this was true as she reflected back on the emptiness she had felt about her book. She knew this was true as she reflected about the coming of autumn.

Elizabeth went to her camp in the woods to be quiet and let the guidance of the universe penetrate her mind and heart and soul. Somewhere she rested in the West, on her journey through the Medicine Wheel, where she needed to find her way.

She had been worried about her spiritual emptiness when she looked at her story board that morning. She realized she had not been taking the time to be alone, to be silent; in fact she had begun to dislike herself for what she saw. She realized she had missed stages of her books development when she was angry on that dog *day of summer*. She knew this because no pictures had meant no poems.

As Elizabeth meditated she became more in touch with her inner life; she was blessed with the greatest lesson of the West. That lesson was to accept herself as she really was, both spiritually and physically, and to never again cut herself off from the spiritual part of her nature. Sarah's timing had been fortuitous. Her friend's questions, a blessing.

The West is a place of sacrifice. Elizabeth looked to where she had come from this year. She looked to the East and saw an innocent and vulnerable human being; it was a place where she had learned humility. She looked to the South and saw the struggles fought to discipline her body and refine her feelings. She saw the pain of love and the heat of conviction on her face; it was here she had received the gift of spiritual insight.

Now, in the West, she learned that for each gift taken, there had to be a sacrifice. She learned if she looked at her life in a spiritual way, she would come to know her place on earth. She received the gift of meditation gladly and what it added to her life on her journey.

Elizabeth went into herself and thought about the year. She remembered the first time she had seen the goose flying north and landing on her lake. She remembered how she had felt a bond to this animal from the start. It was her totem and its timely journey had been her journey, too. Each of them had had to weather great trials, both physically and mentally, in the long northern winter. Each of them had set forth on a new journey with the onset of spring. As the summer had progressed, each had grown with the wisdom of age. Now as the fall approached, they each had to make a spiritual choice again, based now on what their journey had taught them about life. Would they choose to stay in the north, or would the lure of the south lead them to new and unusual, but all too unfamiliar places? Would their lives be ever so entwined? Elizabeth had much meditating to do.

· · ·

The sun had journeyed across the sky and the goose saw some of the families of geese leave the lake every day. She saw more fly in every night. As she now loafed among the tall grasses near the lake, she looked out at her growing family. She had taught them the lessons her instincts had told her to. She taught them what she had learned from the other adults. When they embarked on their journey it would be up to them now to make their own way. Deep inside, her compass was pointing in a new direction. She had responsibilities now. She had communicated this to her gander one evening and he confirmed those instinctive feelings. She knew her young would also begin to feel something too, although they might not comprehend it at first. Why had she ignored those instincts last year?

Soon the goose was distracted, once again, by the antics of the yearlings. She would be glad when next year came and they would start their own families far from her. Of course she also knew that the juveniles would be a year older and had a feeling it would start all over again. She would also have her own juveniles and the number of geese on the lake would increase. Well, not to worry about next year, she had some more teaching to do and had taken a long enough break.

As the goose was swimming toward her fledglings, for their daily flight to the farmer's fields, she looked at the shore. There was the crone with her funny, bulging eyes looking straight back at her. Even after all this time it still made her nervous when the crone grew those bulging eyes. The crone then aimed the one eyed box on the stick at her as she and her family took to the sky, and the goose wondered what she was up to now.

Fall Flight of The Geese

Grandiose aviators

ancestral paths:

magnetic,

polar,

drawing

forth.

Who was first?

How did they know?

ancestral paths:

magnetic,

polar,

drawing

forth.


Grandiose aviators

gathered strength

in summer.

Now

gathered wisdom

in winter.

Now

go.

-Elizabeth Washburn

# Chapter 2

Vermilion, ocher, and gold were casting their woodland dominance and soon only the coniferous trees would add a touch of variation. Looking across the lake and watching the mist rise, Elizabeth anticipated their reflection meeting the spectrum of the rising sun. As she swam in the still lukewarm water she grieved, as she had done so many times this year, for the lost lives of 9/11. She had tears slowly trailing down her face for the fall colors they would never see again. She mourned with the families whose eyes would never appreciate these sights in the same way again.

Stepping onto shore she dried with a velvety towel. Stepping methodically, with a one to one ratio she counted the impending fall chores. Elizabeth would take out last year's list and hope she wouldn't have to add to it.

The day showed signs of being crisp, just like the meteorologist had promised last night. Elizabeth was pleased because she favored dressing in her warmer clothes. She took out her khakis, tee-shirt, and wool shirt, as she had done so many years in the past, and dressed. Putting her hand into her pocket she felt her leather gloves exactly where she had left them last year. She removed her wool shirt and ate pancakes and bacon for breakfast, anticipating a good day's work. Then putting it back on, along with her floppy hat and steel-toed boots, she went down the steps.

Elizabeth opened the steel doors and putting her key into the tractor, the one with the yellow seat, out she went parking it in its spot. Elizabeth was not quite done with the preparation, though, and climbed into her truck and pointed it towards town. About halfway there she stopped at the local fish and game store and was issued a burning permit. She would get a head start on the leaves that had changed and dropped early, by burning them tonight.

Using the blower, Elizabeth went around and around the back yard. Into piles, in the driveway, the leaves built up. Taking only a break for lunch, she devoted herself to this task all day long, reluctantly quitting when she heard the phone ring about 4:30.

. . .

Oh, that woman could talk. Elizabeth had listened politely, then asked her about Carol's boy. "How did he come out on his placement test this fall?" She had tutored him to the best of her ability this summer.

"As fine as John did when you tutored him." Della was referring to the summer Elizabeth had spent twice a week trying to get John caught up a grade. His learning disabilities were almost too severe even for her skills. She took this as a compliment and then told Della she had to put her tools away before nightfall. She couldn't bear to have her launch into another dissertation about that particular subject, or any other.

. . .

The ground looked like a paint-by-number as Elizabeth walked down the trail just a week later. Into her notebook she pressed the golden poplar leaves, the scarlet and cadmium maples, and a couple of sepia colored oak leaves. She would write poems about fall soon, as her publisher was breathing down her neck to finish her chapbook. Into her pockets she put some acorns, and a stick or two into a cloth bag she carried. The stick had to have a knot or other irregularity on it, in just the 'right' place. These, along with the leaves, would be used for a fall arrangement, accompanied by gourds and Indian corn. When Thanksgiving came she would have a natural centerpiece. As she came to her camp, Elizabeth rested on a log as she thought about her friends that would depart soon for Arizona. She decided if she went, this time of the year was too early to go; the leaves were too beautiful and the air too inviting. As she sat and meditated on this dilemma, a wooly caterpillar made its way across the log. Seeing it, she picked it up to look at its stripes. Under close observation she concluded that just as the geese were predicting, it may be a long winter again this year. The squirrels had been gathering acorns already, too, which meant they had been falling early.

Walking to the end of the trail she stopped dead in her tracks. Her totem had also been trying to tell her something but the message just wasn't clear.

. . .


In The Wind Comes Fall

Unnoticed through the summer light,

rippling, surface blue. Floating

like the white and brown, geese

instincts rising through.


Paint by number, still as you fly.

Message in the eye burns true.

Calm the colors as they fall.

Oranges, yellows,

sometimes gray-

in the mind of fall's

decay.

-Elizabeth Washburn


Photographs Fade

Coloration burned

brilliant, but

Fire's soon

going out.

Crackled with

the morning sky;

Painting was washed:

Gamboge,

Scarlet,

Ocher,

Sepia,

Vert.


Age turns to yellow-gray.

-Elizabeth Washburn

# Chapter 3

"We are travelers," the gander communicated to the goose. "Look to the changes in our lives. Our instincts and ancestor stories tell us all there is to know. The young have grown their wings and are now ready to fly. Why do you not keep the teachings of the *Sacred Tree*? Look to the crone as she has found healing, power, wisdom and security; so have you. The journey never ends. We must begin our journey again. The colors fly like the wind as does the water beneath us. Look around you; the other families do not stay."

The goose was the totem, the bearer of these teachings and so also had she learned them. She must remember what the tree had said. She must show the crone the path of the wisdom of the north now as she had done last year. The crone seems to have mastered wholeness. The crone and she are both interrelated with the wind, the animals, the birds, everything in the universe. She is her totem and as the goose does so must the crone. Can she teach her to understand that this need not be the North, the place to seek her wisdom this year?

She had learned what her goslings had taught her. All creation is in a state of constant change. Change is a cyclic pattern. It is not random. It is not by accident. The crone must be taught that the lessons of the East, West, and South were just movements of the change. That everything physical and spiritual is real. Balance honors this reality. Humans are spiritual as well as physical.

"The crone helped her during the cold; is she emotional? The crone carries much with her wings; is she physical? The crone goes to the woods. But does the crone meditate? The meditation period was learned in the West which will soon move into the direction of the North. Must I stay or is my work complete? Will she know what direction to go?"

The goose did not know what the will of the crone would be on her journey. Would they part ways or be forever tied? She knew she would help her on this journey as long as the crone needed her, just as the crone had helped her during the white of the year. She could only fail if one of them did not follow the teachings of the *Sacred Tree*.

. . .

Elizabeth looked into the mirror, the mirror of the Medicine Wheel, to find her inner self. She looked to see if she had the power of her will connected equally to the teachings of each of the four directions, to be able to act on the teachings her totem had shown her. What she saw there appeared to be a mixture of herself the Indian, and herself the crone. She began questioning, for the first time, whether they were compatible; or had she not done herself justice on her journey by paying so much attention to the teachings of the crone. She knew each was a part of her life, but were they in balance? This question had to be answered as she now would enter the North, the direction of Wisdom Walking once again. On this journey she had rediscovered many things and, in the days of the months of the crone, she had celebrated many things. Was she a wise elder as the direction and label of a crone would indicate? Was she the same elder as the four directions would now indicate? Had she completed the journey, once again, to learn more about herself and how to be a wise leader of people?

A crone believes that following the twelve phases is a human ritual celebrating each phase of Earth's great truth. If done, knowledge and life are strengthened. Out of these twelve phases comes one great truth- the unquestionable design of creation, destruction, rebirth- continuing year after year. As an Indian, she believed that following the teachings of the four directions, she had learned the four great meanings of protection, nourishment, growth, and wholeness. Wisdom Walking is a phase that represented both cultures for an elder, a crone.

The sun, which never stops, leads us on our journey of human development, symbolized in the Medicine Wheel. They may be represented by the four grandfathers, the four winds or the four cardinal directions-as Elizabeth thought of the phases. There is a lesson of balance taught when we look into the center and tie the lessons together by the power of our will. As in the poem The Crone, are not the aspects she possesses and rejuvenates each year during the crone ceremonies, related to the lessons of the Four Cardinal Directions? For example: are

225

the teachings of the East, symbolized by the Eagle or the jar of leaves of spring kept by the crone during the ceremony of the New Moon in April? Would the teachings of the West, symbolized by the Black Bear and Turtle or the box of thistles that is burned by the crone after the ceremony for the Autumnal Equinox? Elizabeth was sure, upon reflection, that both aspects of her being were manifestations of each other. Elizabeth used them freely as they were discovered. The greatest lesson she discovered was to accept herself as she really was.

· · ·

The Center

I found

a Horse

that carried me:

the journey.

I found

interconnectedness

of my

being:

the creation.

I found

an Eagle,

a Mouse

showed me:

self-reliance.

I found

a Cougar;

    a Red Willow Tree

gave me

passionate involvement:

with my world.

I found

a Black Bear,

a Turtle

taught me:

*Sacred Tree.*

I found

Great Mountain,

teaching me

how:

I struggled.

The Horse,

she was

a steadfast ride

showed me:

sacred object.

Has the power,

not in itself

but in the

meaning of

the journey?

-Elizabeth Washburn

# Chapter 4

Hunting season opened in October and, for the first time on their flight, the geese barely landed on Elizabeth's lake. Early, as soon as it became light enough to see, the guns were readied in the various blinds. As soon as an unsuspecting duck or flock of geese flew overhead a volley of bird shot was launched toward the sky. If the hunter was good, a duck or goose would fall; sounding to Elizabeth's ears, like a cannon ball a young child might make from the dock. Within an hour of sunrise it would be over for the day and the hunters' soft-mouthed dogs could be seen gathering any downed birds while the extra bird shot slowly sank to the bottom of the lake..

Everyday Elizabeth would rise with the sound and go to see what the mornings take had been. She would get her binoculars and count the geese. She knew there was a limit and was ready to report any hunter she thought had gone over it. She knew most of the hunters on the lake and where they lived.

• • •

The goose and her family were not ignorant of the shotgun. The ancestors had warned of such activities. Unless the day was rainy or foggy, they knew they could fly high enough to evade the shot. But on those days that were not clear, a brother or sister would always fall from the sky. Geese, being very sociable, usually wept for each other and Elizabeth's goose was no exception.

She devised a plan, much against her gander's wishes. Each morning they would hide in the cove where they could not be seen, and eat of the tubers there. Or they would go on shore and into the woods a little ways and just watch. Although it was their nature to seek a farmer's field for their early morning dining pleasure, she was smart enough to have listened to her ancestors.

One morning the gander decided he'd had enough of the antics of the goose and took off on a flight with the fledglings in tow. It was misty that morning, just right for hunting.

· · ·

Elizabeth once again was awakened to the sound of "cannon balls". Although not much consolation, there would only be one more day of it, and she admonished herself for not rising in time to watch the take. There had been much shooting that morning, as she knew there would be, given the conditions. Many gaggles could be heard flying overhead. Everyday she had prayed for the birds, ducks and geese alike, and today was no exception. When daylight hit she counted three ducks and a like number geese. And just like every other day she hoped that her goose was not among them.

· · ·

The goose waited until she could wait no longer. She ran down the water and lifted into the clear morning air. She knew where her family usually went to eat and headed to the farmer's field. Soon she found them. With her high pitched klink-klink she took off, landing back on Elizabeth's lake, and began to weep.

# Chapter 5

The gander had been one of the three. This would cinch the goose's decision. With no mate, and no hope of finding another until the next spring, she would have to join other families flying south for the winter. She could not subject her young to the trials of the north in the winter.

. . .

As the shadows crept across the lawn Elizabeth began by ringing a silver bell four times and lighting the candles in the blackened room.

HOW SHOULD WE CEASE FROM DYING AND FROM SLEEP WHERE WE HAVE TAKEN REFUGE IN DEEP SILENCE? DOTH DEATH ALREADY ROUSE US WITH HIS MUSIC? NO, DEATH HAS NAUGHT TO DO WITH BELLS OR MUSIC. THIS IS A SILVER SOUND, A GHOST OF SOUND, AN ECHO OF SOME LAUGHTER WE HAVE KNOWN-YET WHERE IS LAUGHTER, NOW THAT SUN IS GONE? THIS IS THE SOUND OF LAUGHTER CHANGED TO STONE, AND WARMTH TO FROST, AND FIRE TO REFLECTION: O FEARFUL GHOST! IT IS THE SILVER MOON WHOSE MIRROR TURNS OUR DEATHS UPON THEMSELVES: AS THE TRAPPED CREATURE GNAWS HIS CAPTIVE FLESH, WE WAKEN INTO FRENZY WHILE WE DIE.

She then held the mirror above her head and recited, along with the sage she had invited:

SPIRIT OF NIGHT,
SPECTRE OF SUN,
SCOURGE OF THE DYING,

DOOM OF THE LIVING,
EGG OF THE SERPENT,
WEB OF THE SPIDER,
SERVANT OF DREAMS,
LAMP OF DELUSION
BEACON OF EVIL,
BEARER OF POWER,
CRYSTAL OF KNOWLEDGE,
MIRROR OF MADNESS
ART THOU REDEMPTION?
ART THOU DAMNATION?
SHALL WE ADORE THEE?
SHOULD WE ABHOR THEE?
BRINGEST THOU VISIONS
OF ANGELS OR DEMONS?
SHALL WE REJOICE WITH THEE IN THIS
AWAKENING?
OR SHALL WE FLY FROM THEE TO KIND
DEATH'S COMFORTING?

Then Elizabeth anointed the candles and hands and brows of both of them with jasmine oil while saying another 'poem' of twenty-six lines. When this was finished the four jars containing white wine, anise flavor, corn syrup and extract of almond, were poured over the ice in the large kettle and stirred while saying:

NOW HER GIFT OF FINE CONFUSION
SHALL BE STRENGTHENED IN THIS POTION:
DRINK IT, THAT HER COLD ILLUSION
MAY REDEEM THY MORTAL VISION.

Both of them drank then chanted another twenty-two lines. Finishing, they took a spool of silver thread and tied its end to the silver bell. The sage held the bell while the thread was wound around them both binding each to one another. They then finished with another chant that began:

BOUND IN SILVER WEB, BE FREE;
DYING IN FORMLESS FLAME, NOW LIVE;

and ended with the words:

WHERE NO STING BLINDS,

NO PAIN ASTOUNDS, AND EVEN
IN ANGUISH, NO VOICE SOUNDS.

The ceremony was concluded by the ringing of the bell while the thread was unwound and placed back on the spool. The candles were extinguished while the bell rang until the last was put out. Then the ceremony ended.

Elizabeth removed the items from the table along with the silver cloth that covered it. She undressed; taking off her silver edged black robe of the Sun, Moon, and silver stars. She put back her diamond and crystal ornament she had worn, as well as the silver ribbons. Finally, she went quietly to bed with the full moon shining bright.

# Chapter 6

November 10th brought the first snowfall of any substantial amount. Somehow the geese had known it was blowing in from the West and flew ahead of it that night. The goose and her family joined a gaggle of three other families as they covered the first one-hundred miles south. Elizabeth never noticed that they were gone, as snow always brought about a magnitude of changes.

As she rose the next morning, to a winter that would once again be longer than anyone could imagine, she went to the pole barn to start the John Deere and thought about putting on the snow plow. But what if she went south? As the last of the snowflakes drifted downward she plodded to the pole barn again, got her truck and drove through her driveways, both the upper and lower. She also shoveled a path out to the piles of trees that came down in last summer's storm. This would be enough for people to get through the 3.5 inch snowfall. After finishing, around one o'clock, she ate and readied herself for an afternoon of phone calls.

Elizabeth phoned Hal and John, and Carol. They all said they could come over tomorrow, Saturday, to help Elizabeth burn the windfall. So about 4 p.m. she went to the fish and game store and got a burning permit. Since the snow had fallen, they could burn earlier.

Gathering together on a cold Saturday afternoon, the friends set about their various assigned tasks. Hal had brought his tractor and would push each pile into place so each would flame to a manageable height. The initial flames burst into the sky like Roman Candles outward over Wisdom Lake, (so named by the ancestor), on the fourth of July. Then darkness came, as black smoke followed by gray, turning to hot ash, could be seen for miles as the piles burned down. The few geese that had been caught on the open water last night took off at the sight of the large inferno.

.   .   .

It took the friends working from dusk until nearly 9 every night, Monday, Tuesday and Wednesday to finish the job. Elizabeth provided refreshments and relief as they rotated jobs throughout the evening. Fortunately the snow had been deep enough and the air cold enough that they could finish the job.

Geese came and went during the whole time and it never occurred to Elizabeth that her goose might have been one of the ones that had left. Not until, that is, the first day she had a rest. On that Friday, Elizabeth, rose and went to the spa for a much needed soak. As she relaxed and let the jets massage her back, she gazed out at the lake. She felt something was amiss but didn't know what was causing the uneasy feeling. Trying to shake it off she went and sat in the sauna for about seven minutes, then went into the snow and back. It was while in the snow that she suddenly realized what it was. She hadn't seen any geese on the lake and none near the platform.

Dressing quickly Elizabeth went and got her binoculars. She searched the lake from one shore to the other. She carefully searched the island, where she knew the goose and her family had made their home that spring. She looked toward the cove. Momentarily she thought they could be at the farmers' field, but her instincts told her otherwise. All day long she made futile attempts to locate the family but saw nothing. Finally she told herself not to be ridiculous, because they would be back for their party in the evening.

As evening came, two gaggles flew in. They quickly separated into families and Elizabeth tried to count the number of geese in each. She wasn't quite sure but she thought she counted one of just six. As the sun turned the sky into a brilliant blaze of glory the lead goose ran down the strip and set its wings in motion. One by one, members of the gaggle followed in a spectacular aeronautical display. Sadly, Elizabeth knew what had happened.

.   .   .

"How appropriate," Elizabeth said out loud, "that the ceremony for the dark of the moon in November is here and I am at my lowest point of the year." As she prepared the table with a plain black cloth, a black candle, a large dark flat stone, found on shore, white chalk, incense burner, incense and ointment of the same scent, and a bone of a dead deer, she thought of nothing else but the goose.

At midnight she lit the candle and began the ceremony. Then she unwrapped the bone and spoke some words, not even listening to their meaning, so occupied was her mind with the goose. She likewise went through each step with the various items on the table only coming into focus again at the conclusion, when she heard herself say:

NOT EVEN EVER MORE **FAREWELL**:

NOT EVEN EVER MORE **FAREWELL**:

NOT EVEN EVER MORE **FAREWELL**.

As Elizabeth blew the candle out and the ceremony came to an end, signifying the death of the year, Elizabeth bade the goose farewell in her heart.

. . .

Letters and phone calls came almost every week now, all asking the same questions, "When can we expect you and will you stay till spring?" Most of them stated they had found the 'perfect' place for Elizabeth to stay, or some even more aggressively stating, 'to buy.'

"Hello, Elizabeth, it's Sarah."

"Oh no, have you phoned with that same old question again?"

"Well, that's a fine greeting! Actually, no. I was phoning to tell you I've decided that you needed me there, so I'm flying up next week. We'll have some good old fashion 'girl talk' and I can find out what this fascination with winter is all about. Can you drive to the cities and pick me up at the airport?"

"Well, this is certainly a surprise! Of course I can. When are you coming? What airline? What flight? When will you be arriving?"

"I'll be arriving on December 18th on Northwest flight 101. It arrives at 4:10 p.m. Sorry about the time of day. I know it will put us back at the lake rather late."

"Well, maybe I should splurge and get us a room in town for the night?"

"You know I don't have a lot of warm clothes down here, why don't we just stay at my place for the night? Then I can pick up some winter clothing," Sarah said, hopefully.

"Of course, just what was I thinking," Elizabeth lied just a little. She really liked her bed.

"Then it's all set; I'll see you on the 18th."

"I'll be there."

"Goodbye Elizabeth."

"So long Sarah."

Elizabeth began making preparations right away; the onset of an early winter had set her arthritis off, but the slow deliberate steps she had been experiencing disappeared. The sheets got changed. The furniture was dusted. And the floors vacuumed. She looked liked she was in the East, not the North, of the cycle.

Elizabeth thought about all the phone calls; depressing phone calls, too. She knew that her friends were right. She should be in Arizona; if not for the long winters, then for her health. If she was so thankful that Sarah was coming, well, maybe they were right. Now maybe once and for all she could make a good decision.

• • •

Sarah arrived, as planned, on that Monday. She had only an overnight bag with her, and a light jacket on. Elizabeth, anticipating this, had brought one of her extra coats, even though she knew it would be way too large for Sarah. Seeing her at the airport put the largest smile on Elizabeth's face, one that had not been there in over a month.

"Hi. How was your flight?"

"Just fine. We left and arrived on time, which is a miracle in this day and age."

"Is that all you brought?"

"Everything else that I'll need will be at the house. Thanks for the coat. I was anticipating freezing when the pilot said it was only 18 degrees."

"Yes, well you know how it is here, unpredictable."

The friends chatted all the way to Sarah's, catching up on the latest gossip. Sarah told Elizabeth how Pat had a new boyfriend and they had a belly laugh over that. Pat had already been married and divorced three times. Sarah had been reading <u>Blind Descent</u> by Nevada Barr and highly recommended it to Elizabeth. Elizabeth mentioned that her book was almost ready for publication. She only had to put the finishing touches on it.

· · ·

Over the next couple of days there was no talk of Arizona or Wisconsin. The friends enjoyed each others' company, whether it was eating chili or listening to Garrison Keillor. On the twenty-first they performed the ceremony for the Winter Solstice. What a joy this was, to be together, since the ceremony bore the greatest significance of all during the year. It resolved the paradox of death and subsequent rebirth. With the leader, in this case Sarah, going out the door followed by Elizabeth, as the ceremony came to the end, they left twelve red candles to burn down. As the ceremony ended, the universal cycle was renewed.

The next day Sarah broke the news.

"I've taken the liberty of booking a flight for you on the 24th with me. Now, before you say no, listen to what I have to say. I've found a little place you can take for three months. Just until April, when spring is supposed to return here. Its cost is reasonable, it has no maintenance, and it is close to four different retirement communities, all of which have new homes for sale. You don't have to worry about a car because Pat is living with her new boyfriend and she said you can use hers. I know how you are suffering with that arthritis and the hot desert air will do it good. You can try the hiking, if your knees permit, the plays, and the sights. I've freed my calendar for most of those three months. And we would all love to have you for Christmas. Please, Elizabeth, don't say no. Give it time to sink in. I'll ask you for your answer tomorrow."

"Fair enough," was all Elizabeth could manage.

· · ·

Elizabeth got little sleep that night. As dawn broke she had her answer.

When Sarah rose that morning Elizabeth already had the coffee made. It had snowed lightly the night before making everything seem soft and alive. The snowbirds sang and deer tracks were the only flaw on the pure whitewashed landscape. Sarah poured herself a cup of that first morning coffee and sat in Elizabeth's chair. Elizabeth had already taken the sofa for herself and was curled up with her pen and paper. She handed the paper to Sarah as if passing a note in a classroom. Both women put down their coffee as Sarah read the few words.

<u>*Dawn*</u>

*Each morning rising.*

*After sleep, give thanks for life.*

*Accept who I am.*

-*Elizabeth Washburn*

Placing the haiku on the table between them, Sarah looked at Elizabeth knowingly and said, "All endings are not found in new beginnings."

• • •

Grasping the poem in her hand, Elizabeth said, "Good-bye," to Sarah, and watched her taillights disappear.